SPECTACLE

Part One – The Spectacle Trilogy

A Young Adult, Science-Fiction Series

S.J. Pierce

Foundations, LLC.
Brandon, MS 39047
www.foundationsbooks.net

Spectacle
By: S.J. Pierce

Cover by: Wit and Whimsy
Edited by: Toni Michelle
Copyright 2015© S.J. Pierce

Published in the United States of America
Worldwide Electronic & Digital Rights
Worldwide English Language Print Rights

This is a work of fiction. Names, characters, businesses, places, events, and incidents are either the products of the author's imagination or used in a fictitious manner. Any resemblance to actual persons, living or dead, or actual events is purely coincidental.

All rights reserved. No part of this book may be reproduced, scanned or distributed in any form, including digital and electronic or mechanical, including photocopying, recording, or by any information storage and retrieval system, without the prior written consent of the Publisher, except for brief quotes for use in reviews

ISBN-13: 978-1985169425
ISBN-10: 1985169428

For Annie Ruth

Table of Contents

Chapter 1 11

Chapter 2 19

Chapter 3 27

Chapter 4 34

Chapter 5 41

Chapter 6 48

Chapter 7 53

Chapter 8 58

Chapter 9 64

Chapter 10 70

Chapter 11 75

Chapter 12 81

Chapter 13 87

Chapter 14 93

Chapter 15 98

Chapter 16 103

Chapter 17 108

Chapter 18 114

Chapter 19 122

Chapter 20 128

Chapter 21 133

Chapter 22 140

Next in the series:... 147
About the Author:..148
Other Titles Available from this Author......................149
Other Titles Available from Foundations, LLC........... 152

"She's seen the horrors of hell; she's endured the darkest of times. It made her hard. She now walks with the fierceness of the wolf. She lives with the bravery of the lion. And acts with the fierceness of the dragon."

-Jordan Sarah Weatherhead, Author of "Naked Truth"

PART ONE:

THE ISLAND

Chapter 1

Dusty Fulmer is an a-hole. A scrawny, stupid a-hole. And he has bad breath.

I know I shouldn't use the 'a' word... or hint at the use of it. My dad would kill me. But there's never a truer word to describe someone like him. I could go on and on all day with reasons why, but what irks me the most, what makes my blood burn hot, is how he treats my friend Jacks.

But Dusty's about to get what's coming to him.

"Stay down," I instruct Jackson, Jacks for short.

He's quivering beside me. I really need to teach him to have a backbone. "We don't have to do this, Mira," he says all mouse-like and pushes his glasses back up his nose. "I wasn't even hungry at lunch. Apparently, he needed the money."

"Trust me," I hiss. "He doesn't need lunch money more than you." Dusty's father is the mayor of our sector and the richest. Not that it will matter soon, according to my father. Food is already being rationed out at the local markets, regardless of who has the means to buy more.

Behind the bushes, we wait. Sweat covers our skin from the blistering, dry air. My tank top clings like a wet blanket, and Jacks' glasses are fogged over. Ninety-five degrees today, our teacher said.

He wipes a bead of sweat traveling along his freckled cheek. "Really, Mira... it's-"

"Shhh!" I say, swatting. "He's going for it."

We stiffen.

Hold our breaths.

As Scrawny Dusty heads for the bait – a duffle bag conveniently left beside the only tree on the front lawn of our school – I wonder if we shouldn't go through with it. Not because he doesn't deserve it; he shouldn't be picking on a kid like Jacks. Especially a kid with Muscular Dystrophy. Maybe we shouldn't go through with it because we could get in trouble... *big* trouble. *Too late now,* I think as Dusty squats and reaches for the zipper. I knew he'd go for it.

This was just too easy.

Jacks inhales sharply and winces, waiting for what comes next.

Dusty unzips the bag.

I watch with an evil grin.

Puff. The homemade stink bomb explodes in his face. As Dusty writhes and sputters and cries like a two-year-old, Jacks and I cover our mouths to smother our giggles. Oh, the gleeful satisfaction of seeing a jerk like him suffer, if only for a few minutes.

We wait for Dusty to stagger home. When he's out of sight, we move from behind our leafy veil. I stretch my legs and help Jacks stand. Frowning internally, I notice how much weaker he seems today. His disease will slowly but surely confine him to a wheelchair. We're only ten.

That was the only thing keeping me from jumping out of the bushes and teasing Dusty after the bomb went off – he'd want to chase us, and Jacks wouldn't be able to keep up.

Spectacle

I scan the schoolyard. Nobody. Knowing Dusty hangs out after school to look for more trouble to get into, we stayed late as well. I'm sure our parents are on the phone now asking if the other's child made it home. "Home?" I ask, shrugging his book bag onto my shoulder. He doesn't protest this time; he must feel as weak as he looks. The heat isn't helping.

"Sure," he replies, and we start on our way.

Our hands clasped tight, Jacks and I thread through the crowded sidewalk, and I'm all but suffocating. Too many people. Some are milling around, some heading somewhere with purposeful strides. It would be easy for two small kids to get lost. Except, we don't. We know these streets well; we walk them home from school every day.

Cars are reserved for the ones with a lot of money, like Dusty Fulmer's family. The government charges hefty fines to own one. They say it's to keep pollution down... and because they can. I hear before the Great Disaster – the day the Earth changed – cars were plentiful and made in places called factories. Cars today are made from leftover parts and hand-built in garages. Another reason they're expensive. And the main reason we don't own one.

Fifteen minutes later, we arrive at our building. Last year, it only took us ten. Either Jacks is getting slower, which I don't want to admit, or the sidewalks are getting more crowded. Could be both.

The cool air from inside blows the hair from my shoulders as we enter. I imagine this is what Heaven is like – a soft, breezy reprieve. Hell is outside.

"See you tomorrow," I say as we stop at his door – Unit 1B. A bony cat rushes by. Chasing a mouse, I'm sure.

Jacks takes his bag and gives me one of his toothy grins. "Bye, Mira."

"Bye," I say, tousling his messy brown hair. *Who could ever pick on you?* I wonder and watch him limp his way inside.

I fiercely hope Dusty is still gagging from the stink bomb.

An unfamiliar smell fills our apartment – cheese and... I inhale... chicken, I think, and something foreign. A few *somethings foreign*.

My nose crinkles.

Blech. Mom's experimenting with casseroles again. I hope my dog, Trevor, is hungry; he'll be getting most of mine under the table.

I find her in our tiny kitchen, her dark hair pulled into a high bun, her tattered apron tight around her hips, but her smile is off. Strained.

Uh oh. She knows about Dusty.

My stomach drops.

"Hey, sweetie," she says sadly, kissing my hair.

Well... maybe she doesn't.

"Hey," I reply cautiously.

She takes my bag from my shoulder. "Get washed up. Dinner will be ready in five."

I nod my reply and head for my room.

"And, Mirabella?"

"Yes?" I call from the hallway.

"Don't disturb your father. He's... not well today. He's resting."

She is *so* lying. I can tell by the way her voice trembles. Dad says pure spirits can't handle dark things like deceit. He always knows when mom and I are fibbing. "Yes, mom."

Trevor makes excited circles around my feet as I wash my hands in our only bathroom. Rust tinges the water again. Old water heaters, management tells us. Nothing we should worry about. Looks gross, though.

I change into a pair of cotton shorts and a clean tank top and meet mom in the kitchen. She jumps, swipes away a tear, and forces another smile. She wasn't expecting me back so soon.

Spectacle

"Iced tea?" she asks a little too cheerily, and heads for the fridge, but it looks more like she's escaping. She's afraid I'll ask what's wrong.

So, I don't. "Sure," I reply.

I notice our radio isn't on. She always listens to it while she's cooking. Our curtains are drawn tight as well.

"Hear anything interesting today?" she asks, pulling out my chair. The ice inside my glass clinks as she fills it with tea. Her hands are shaking.

"No," I say, which is true. The only thing that seemed out of place was when Jacks and I passed the market. People were arguing with the clerks about how many loaves of bread they were allowed to buy now.

"Good," my mom breathes. She looks relieved. Did she *expect* me to hear something? I don't ask.

Dinner is quiet and hurried, but I clean my plate like a good daughter, Trevor's belly fuller than mine. Mom doesn't say why my father isn't joining us. Again, I don't pry. I clear the table and start on the dishes like always. Then it's homework, shower, and bed.

And, without my parents' knowledge, the rooftop. I've been looking forward to it all day.

Far past my bedtime, I read under my covers with a flashlight, occasionally stopping and listening for my parents' fevered whispering to end. They've been up talking forever.

I make out a couple of words – something about how much they think I can handle. It doesn't make any sense, so I return to my reading.

Mom insists I read a book a week, even if it's poetry. She says idle minds turn to mush. At first, I resisted, but over time, I've adopted her love of words, specifically her love for poetry. I adore how the words swing and swirl to their own rhythm, like songs too beautiful and important for music to accompany them. The first time she handed me a book of poetry, she told me, "Sip every word slowly and ponder its meaning. Every line will etch its name on your heart." At first, I didn't understand what she meant, but now, after reading and rereading several of them, I do. A man named Robert Frost is my favorite. Virginia Woolf is a close second. I also like Keats.

Once my parents' whispering morphs into snores, I put my book away and sneak out the front door to the stairwell leading to the rooftop. I should have remembered my jacket – it can be breezy and cool up here at night – but I don't care. I'm outside. Just me and the moon and the stars.

I'm free.

I settle in my spot beside the ledge facing east, and the moon, full and orange tonight, gives me an eerie feeling. Soft, nearly invisible rings are circling it again. I often wonder if they appear because there's a certain haze to the atmosphere, a thickness. And I don't know how or why, but something bad always happens the next day. It's like the moon and I have some twisted, secret understanding, except the moon knows all the details and I'm left with a bad taste in my mouth. It'll be hard to enjoy my night up here now.

I look to the stars for comfort. I've always felt a connection there. Like we are one, somehow. Like I am from them and they are from me. Dad says I love them because I have a star-shaped birthmark on my forearm; the same birthmark his mother had. I wish I'd known her.

My mind drifts to my favorite Frost poem:
O Star (the fairest one in sight),
We grant your loftiness the right
To some obscurity of cloud –
It will not do to say of night,
Since dark is what brings out your li-
"Pssst... Mira," a voice whispers.
I squeak.
"*Shhh.* It's me," he says.
Luxxe. My other best friend.
"What are you doing out here?" I ask, part happy to see him, part irritated. This is *my* spot. My quiet time.

Spectacle

"Just seeing what you do up here every night," he teases. "Thought maybe there was some big secret I was missing out on."

"This is it," I say with a shrug.

He plants himself beside me, and we stare up at the sky together. "Spooky looking moon," he adds.

We sit in silence, and my gaze rakes over the jagged mountains lifting over the horizon. The ocean lies beyond them; I've wanted to fly over them many times with my father. He's a government pilot who flies with a team of others in constant search of new land. Their theory is when the earthquakes happened, a shelf containing water below the Earth's surface sprang free, causing a great flood. That was two hundred years ago. They hope one day the water will slowly recede back to where it came from and expose more land for us to live on.

Dad says he hasn't found much yet. Nothing inhabitable, unfortunately. Until then, what's left of the human race will remain huddled on the three remaining continents. We live in New America, the smallest of them. Our homeless rate has tripled in the past year, which doesn't help with the crowded streets. Sometimes, we'll find homeless people under our stairwells and bring them whatever food we can spare, which isn't much. Dad says it's the right thing to do.

Dad. I hope he's okay.

Luxxe sighs. "Is this really what you do up here?"

"Well, go then..." I say, bumping into him. Boys, so impatient. And Luxxe always has to be in constant motion.

He stays, and I notice his jaw is strained. Worry fills his eyes. Not him too...

"What's wrong?" I finally ask.

His lips pull down, and he kicks around a dead moth. I think he mumbles, "Nothing."

I wait a moment, then say, "Tell me."

His dark eyes search mine, looking for something, but I don't know what. He then seems disappointed that he doesn't find that *something* there. What is *with* everyone today?

"I think I'll go." He yawns his words, but not a true yawn. The forced yawn he does when he fakes being tired, so he can go home. "Bye, Mira."

"Bye," I say, and he hugs me harder than normal. I watch him leave, the wind up here tossing his black curls around. They're almost invisible at night from this distance, except for the moonlight dancing on each one as they move.

I know this sounds weird, but he reminds me of my father – his dark hair and eyes, broad nose, and olive skin. Like they're related, somehow. He would fit perfectly in our family portraits. Unlike me. You'd think I'm someone else's with my pale skin and hair and light blue eyes. I can't even say I look like my mother. My parents' friends joke that I'm the milkman's daughter. I have no idea what that means.

Once he disappears down the stairwell, I return to stargazing, trying to avoid the rings around the moon and worrying why they're there.

My gut tells me it might have to do with my father. And Luxxe.

Chapter 2

I awake to my bed jostling, a wet tongue dragging across my cheek. *Trevor.*

"Time to get up, Mirabella," mom calls by my door, then turns for the living room.

I stretch and rumple Trevor's already messy salt-and-pepper fur. He licks my arm in return. After he curls against my belly, I wait for dad to come get him as he usually does. They both go on morning strolls before dad leaves for work, but he never comes.

"Mira... get up," mom calls again.

She shortened my name this time. I better listen.

I pull my long hair up, dress quickly, and feed Ryder, my chameleon, before heading to the kitchen. Dad bought him for me last Christmas. I'd begged him to get me one since I was old enough to speak. They said I'd seen one in a picture book and fell in love with their "googly eyes." I don't remember the book, or calling them googly eyes, but I do remember always having a love for them. I wear one carved out of moonstone around my neck.

Following the scent of cheese toast and eggs, I stop short when I see my mom standing in the kitchen doorway, her hands fidgeting with the frayed hem of her apron, that same tight smile on her face. I don't like this new way she looks at me — worried and afraid and about to cry all at the same time. "Mirabella, dear," she says, almost whimpers. "Daddy and I need to talk to you."

Heat crawls over my skin, flushing my cheeks and leaving gooseflesh on my arms. Dread squeezes my lungs. "Okay," I manage, but it takes me a minute to remember how to walk. Mom doesn't move out of my way.

I notice the radio isn't on again. Dad usually listens to it for his morning news.

She kneels to look me at me on my level, and I know now something really bad must have happened... or is happening. Yet again, the rings around the moon were right.

"Everything's okay," she lies, reading my worried expression, "But I want to warn you about your father before you see him."

My eyebrows draw together. *Warn me?*

I hear dad shifting in his chair, and he grunts nervously. My chest clenches tighter. All I want is to see him. To know what's going on. I can't fathom what she would have to warn me about.

"His skin is... *different* than before."

"Different?"

"Yes, baby," she soothes. "And whatever you do, please don't scream. You know how thin these walls are."

I muster a nod.

"Okay," she says, clasping my hand and straightening, "It's time."

She leads me into the kitchen, my heart racing, my eyes snapping right to my father. He's sitting with his face behind his hands, elbows resting against the tabletop. The skin on his arms and hands look the same to me — smooth and the color of coffee with milk. Still normal. I breathe a sigh of relief.

"Is she looking?" he asks through his hands.

Spectacle

I answer for her. "Yes, daddy."

He lets out a long slow breath – a brooding sigh.

"Show her, Grant," mom pleads.

Moments pass. He sighs again and slowly moves his hands away. Behind them, blue marks, starting at the corners of his eyes, branch out in a rough, jagged pattern - like webs of blood vessels, but more defined - over his cheekbones and stopping along his jawline. Smaller patches curl around his temples. It almost looks like a butterfly, almost beautiful, like these odd markings are meant to be there. Like someone had painted them for fun. I would assume this is all a joke had my mom not been acting so weird.

I look up to her questioningly. Why would this have made me scream?

Her hand meets her chest, and I can tell she's relieved I didn't freak out, but not all the concern is gone from her eyes. At least she's smiling normally now.

"You aren't afraid?" she asks.

"Why would I be?"

Her lips press tight. She throws a nervous glance at my father.

"Because these are permanent," he says. "And they'll get worse."

I consider what he said for a moment, and worry seizes me again. Permanent? *Worse?* Does this mean he's sick?

"It's normal, though," he assures me.

I frown. Why is he lying to me? I'm old enough to know that blue marks on peoples' faces aren't normal.

"Normal for *me*," he adds.

"Don't lie, daddy," I say, crossing my arms, "I'm not stupid."

"I'm serious, pumpkin."

My lips purse and I make my way to him. I take a napkin, dip it in a glass of water on the table and rub it in circles over the blue marks. They stay put. I look at the napkin. Clean.

"I told you," he says, his words heavy with sadness.

I study the marks closer. They should probably frighten me, as my parents anticipated, but they don't. They somehow seem normal. Expected. I don't know why.

"Let's go to your room and talk a little more," he suggests, cupping my face in his hands. It could be my imagination, but the blue marks along his jaw have stretched toward his chin in these few short minutes. They're spreading as he said. They're getting worse.

"Okay," I say timidly, and he ushers me away.

We sit on the edge of my bed, my feet dangling. Dad had taken Ryder out of his aquarium and placed him on his finger.

Mom is leaving us to our privacy. She must know everything he's planning to say.

"So, Mira," he begins, studying Ryder as he slowly crawls toward the back of his hand. His googly eyes search all around. "What can you tell me about this little guy? What makes him so special?"

"Well... he's cute," I say, and I realize I'm clasping my chameleon pendant as I study dad's blue markings.

He chuckles. "Yes, baby. What else?"

"He changes colors when he feels threatened."

Flashing an approving smile, he says, "Exactly." He pauses reflectively. "What if I were to tell you I'm not so different from Ryder?"

I can't help but trace one of the markings on dad's cheek with my finger. "You mean because of these?"

"Right."

I don't understand.

"These blue markings are my true form. I was born like this."

My jaw falls. "You... you were?"

"Yes. In a place far, far away from here."

I try to decipher what he means. "Like on one of the other two continents?"

Spectacle

A shadow passes over his expression, and I know it's somewhere he doesn't want to say. He chews on the inside of his cheek like he does when he thinks too hard.

"Just say it, dad."

Rubbing the tension from his neck, he answers. "Further away than that. Think *further*."

Further? I shrug and take Ryder from my dad, so I can hold him. "I don't know."

"Use your imagination," he coaxes.

Further...

It hits me like a ton of bricks. "Like, not on this planet?"

He gives me a slow, cautious nod. "Yes, baby."

The revelation overwhelms me, and my heart skips, my stomach stirring. Yet, at the same time, the idea seems as normal to me as his markings. Familiar, in a way, yet foreign. "How is that...? How did you...?"

He rests a hand on my knee to calm me. "It's a long story, pumpkin. One I'll have to explain later, in further detail."

"Now," I plead. "Please tell me."

He sighs, eyeing me, looks to the door, then back to me. Did mom not want me to know yet?

"*Please?*"

Lowering his voice, he says, "Okay..." He clears his throat. "All you need to know is I traveled here from another planet when I was younger. Around sixteen years old."

He watches me, hoping that crumb of information will cap my curiosity. No such luck. I wait patiently. I want more.

Reluctantly, and quieter, he continues. "It was overtaken by a more brutal..." He searches for the right words, or *appropriate* words, for my age. "...ruthless race of beings, only interested in the resources on our planet. We had no chance of winning, so most of the tribes, around a hundred thousand of us, were able to escape in some of their pods, which were pre-programmed to head for Earth next. We crashed into Earth's ocean at nightfall, and after all was said and done, a good number of us died. Around twenty thousand or so."

I blink at him as I take it all in; brutal race of beings... escaped in pods... crashed into the ocean. Many of them died. "Twenty thousand?"

"Yes, Mira," he replies, gently squeezing my knee, "And even more died as we swam toward land. It was a long way for some of them."

"So how many made it?" My voice is as soft as a whisper now. Like the fluttering of a moth's wings. If I pinch myself, will I wake from some frightening, bizarre, impossibly beautiful dream? This is *way* better than any book I've read. I almost want him to stop, but I have to know. I just have to.

"We estimated around half. Fifty thousand or so."

"Did anyone see you? With your blue markings, I mean?"

"Once we made it to land, a man walking along the shoreline found those of us who hadn't already started our way inland."

"What did he think of your skin?"

Dad strokes Ryder's back. "He didn't know. By the time he got close enough to see us, we were able to change our skin to look like his, and all our blue markings were hidden deep inside."

"You changed the color of your skin," I muse. "Like Ryder."

"Right. For self-preservation. We didn't know what this human's race was capable of or how they'd treat unexpected visitors to their planet." He picks Ryder up again and puts him back in his cage. It's not good to hold him long. "That's my point to this conversation. My species are considered Changers. We can adapt our skin to our surroundings. We can also speak any language after hearing someone else speak a few words."

I test the word. "Changers." *Cool.* "Can I see?"

He beams at me, a proud, thoughtful look. "Sure." His hand rests on my polka-dotted comforter, then morphs to the same light purple, perfect black spots trickling up his fingers.

I gape, awestruck. "What else can you do?"

"That's really about it."

I try to hide my disappointment. "Well, what happened next?" I still want more.

Spectacle

"The tribal Elders, what was left of them, told him we were shipwreck survivors, that our fishing boats had gotten caught in a bad storm. Which, technically, we kind of were shipwreck survivors, but thankfully, the space pods we'd arrived in were long gone and at the bottom of the ocean somewhere. The man offered us help, to go get authorities, but we kindly refused, and he went on his way.

Once we regrouped, those of us left without parents were taken in by the adults, and we all had to find our own ways of blending in with society here."

"Who took *you* in?"

"The Elder of my tribe, Amara. She raised me until I was old enough to be on my own. Because of her, I was able to go to school, become a pilot and have a family of my own."

Amara. I've never heard of her before. "Why don't I know her?"

The lines on his forehead deepen. Mentioning her must have opened wounds inside. I can tell he loved her. *Loves* her. Misses her deeply. "She passed before you were born."

Oh.

"And grandma?" I knew she passed away long ago, but they told me it was because she was in an accident.

"She..." He swallows hard, tears shimmering in his eyes, "She didn't make it, baby. The bad guys got her before we escaped."

I take a moment to grieve for this woman I never knew. This woman I supposedly look like. Now that I know more about her, how she died and why, it makes her more real to me. Not just some person he's mentioned before in stories. I feel robbed.

Needing comfort, I wilt into my dad's side. He wraps an arm around me and pulls me tighter. We stay like this for a while.

I break the heavy silence. "But the blue marks, why are you showing them now?"

"I'm not choosing to," he says. "Apparently, our skin can only hold its camouflage for so long before our true selves shoulder their way back through. That goes for anything, really. Secrets and lies can only stay hidden for so long before the truth breaks its shackles and sets itself free. There's no fighting it."

I nod in agreement, although I don't fully understand the weight of this concept. I suppose I haven't lived long enough to.

"And I'm not the only one. I've called around to the others. They're changing too."

"Who are they?"

"You already know some of them," he says, and sadness fills his voice again. "Jacks' and Luxxe's parents."

I gasp. *What?* I remember Luxxe's expression last night. He must have known already and was hoping I did too. He must have wanted to talk.

"What about mom?" She doesn't have markings.

"She's human. I shared all of this with her a long time ago."

She knew. Mom knew this entire time. I somehow feel robbed by that too, though I understand why they didn't tell me. It needed to stay a secret, for some reason. What that reason is, makes me uneasy.

"What will people say?" I ask, my voice shaking, "Is that why you haven't left for work? Why our curtains are closed?"

"Yes, baby," he says, stroking my hair, "People are already starting to speculate. Some think we're sick. That we have a disease we're going to spread. Some people think we might be cursed. A few of us are going to ask to speak with Mayor Fulmer to tell him the truth. Open his eyes to what happened around twenty-five years ago."

"What do you think he'll say?"

"I don't know, Mira," he says, kissing my forehead and standing, "But I hope he's open-minded... if he agrees to speak with us."

By the time he leaves my room, the blue markings are already trickling down his neck.

Chapter 3

I haven't been to school in a week. More and more Changers have blue marks, and more and more rumors are swirling. Even though I don't have the marks myself, kids at school found out my dad has them, so that made me a target too. Dad says people get angry at things they don't understand because they're afraid. It's how they deal. I understand what he means; I've experienced it. Mom pulled me out of school when Francine cut a chunk of my hair off. She said she was going to send it to a lab and have it inspected for the "Blue Disease."

That's what they're calling it, even on the news. We don't turn the radio on anymore because dad gets angry. He yells at it and calls them "ignorant jerks."

"Things will change today when we meet with the mayor," he says, wiggling the knot of his tie into place. His hands have the blue marks on them now. Everything on him has markings, except the soles of his feet. "Once everyone's enlightened, they'll understand what's happening. There's nothing to be afraid of."

I'm not so sure.

People seem pretty frightened to me. Someone pelted Jacks' mom in the head with a rock the other day. She needed stitches but refused to go to the hospital. Will that go away once they learn it's because the Changers are from another planet?

I'm not frightened, but it does look strange to me, seeing his entire body marked up like someone drew on him with careful, artistic strokes. And maybe it's the part of me that's half Changer, but somehow, it still seems familiar. Like this is the way he's always been. He definitely has a way about him now, a comfort in this skin. More so than before. Like a tiger finally being able to show the stripes he'd hidden for so long. I'm still not sure if I like it or not.

According to dad, I better get used to it. None of them can change back, not to their human coloring anyway, and more than likely, since I'm half Changer, I'll probably get my markings around sixteen – the Age of Ascent, as his people call it. My people too, I suppose. It marks the time I make the climb into adulthood.

I'm not ready for any of that.

"I'll see you ladies, shortly," he says, sparing one last look in the mirror by the front door. "Need to meet William and Jacob in the lobby."

William and Jacob – Jacks' and Luxxe's dads. I only caught pieces of my parent's conversation this morning, but apparently, they snuck into William's office building last night and coordinated a conference call with other Changers to appoint three representatives for today's meeting. Since dad, William, and Jacob are all offspring of – or had been raised by – tribal Elders, they were nominated.

Before he disappears through the door, he kisses both our heads as we piece together a puzzle on the coffee table. Mom needs something to do to quell the anxiety until he returns, and neither of us is centered enough to read. Rock-throwing is tame compared to other things going on outside.

When I make my rooftop visits now, sirens mostly fill the air.

Spectacle

When dad returns, he wears a triumphant grin – the first time we've seen a smile in this apartment since all of this began. My mother launches herself into his arms. I think she cries a little too, but she hides her face from me, so I can't be sure.

"Good news," he crows, releasing her and bending to kiss my hair again, "The mayor seemed receptive to what we had to say. He's taking it to President Howell."

"Then what?" mom prods, wiping her wet cheeks. Yes, she's definitely crying.

"If we can get the government's full support, they'll release a statement and have this entire thing put to rest."

With a hopeful glint in her eye, her hand meets her chest, and she takes a broken breath. "Well, what did he say about what you are? Did he freak out at first?"

"He seemed pretty calm, actually. I think compared to other things they'd assumed, this is the least harmful to society. We simply sought refuge here. That's all. We're different, but not harmful."

"So, you really think thi-" Mom chokes on her words, the relief and joy too much to bear, and dad pulls her into another hug. My eyes sting with tears as I watch them.

"Yes, love. I really think things will get better."

I stare at my reflection in my patent leather shoes. I don't like my hair cropped this short, but I had no choice thanks to Francine. I also don't like wearing this frilly dress or pearl necklace. I clutch my moonstone chameleon in my dress pocket. I couldn't bear leaving it behind, and it makes me feel better to have it near.

I'm nervous about today.

My gaze shifts out the taxi window. We're in the only part of town that doesn't belong to a sector, the buildings partially demolished long ago by the earthquakes. They look more like rubble now, the ruins of some ancient society with weeds and twisting vines squeezing through every possible crevice. The road is bumpier here too, though still mostly maintained since we have to drive through here to get to the capital.

They teach us in school that the capital used to be a place called Washington, D.C., and the President lived in a big white mansion called the White House. It now lies entombed in rubble beneath the ocean's surface, miles and miles away from here, and the new capital is in the remains of what was once Denver, Colorado. In the part that wasn't destroyed.

The ruins-slash-jungle morphs into whole buildings and fenced-in trees, and I know we have to be close. This part of town is all manicured squares of grass, shiny glass buildings and expensive-looking cars. More cars than I've seen my entire life. I can't help but press my face against the window.

After multiple stops where men in dark green uniforms check my parents' IDs and search the car, we pull into a parking garage. More men in uniforms wait outside our doors.

"They're only here to escort us in," mom assures me. I don't like how big and mean they look, but her relaxed smile eases me. She truly believes we're safe, so we must be. "And remember your manners," she adds before exiting.

I follow and sidle up to her. We wait for Jacks' and Luxxe's taxis to park so we can walk together. We were all invited to come today to stand behind the President in a press conference as he addresses our small nation. It will be broadcast on radio and TV... for those who can afford them. Today, he's declaring our race equal, and we're to be treated as such. Nobody is to discriminate or commit hate crimes.

We've been accepted into New America with open arms. And why wouldn't we be? As dad says, we've been contributing as decent citizens for nearly two decades already. We'd proven ourselves as hardworking and trustworthy before we ever knew there would be a need to.

Walking close to mom as we follow the big men inside, I glance at Jacks and Luxxe. They look funny in their fancy suits, all dressed up and penguin-like. I giggle. Luxxe points at me and does the same. I stick out my tongue.

Two more security checks and we're finally inside the tallest building in the city – capital headquarters, or as some call it, the new White House. Inside, it's like a dream – glittering marble floors with swirls of grey and cheerful lighting. We stop at a curved marble desk, slightly darker than the floor, and the New American flag – with fifteen stars to represent each sector – proudly hangs on the wall behind it.

From behind the desk, a sharply dressed lady exchanges words with the big men, and then she escorts us to an elevator. After swiping her badge, she flashes a courteous smile and leaves us.

I swallow hard, thinking about meeting the President soon, and as if she senses my growing panic, mom slides her hand into mine. Nothing to be afraid of, I remind myself. Today is a good day. Today, the kids at school are no longer allowed to be mean to me and I don't have to worry about dad every time he leaves.

But something irks me, and I remember looking out my bedroom window last night. Those stupid rings had shown up again around the moon. I try to forget them. "They mean nothing," I whisper to myself, willing it to be. They mean nothing.

Unbidden, my thoughts conjure a poem:
So blend the turrets and shadows there
That all seems pendulous in air
While from a proud tower in the town
Death looks gigantically down...

I stop before I freak myself out. Edgar Allen Poe always finds a way into my thoughts when I'm on edge.

We wait in a room with leather couches and a snack buffet. If a mouse sneezes, I'll hear it. Nobody says a word. We're all nervous, I guess. My dad keeps glancing at the clock. Fifteen minutes pass. Thirty.

"Must be running late," William says, his gravelly voice cutting through the silence. He strokes his beard anxiously.

"I'm sure that's it," Jacob echoes.

My dad doesn't look so sure.

We wait some more, and I grow fidgety. Mom hands me a piece of paper to draw on, and I sketch a picture of Trevor. She praises it quietly, but I know it's no good; it looks like a mop with stick legs. Luxxe laughs at it, and I crumple it up, fantasizing about throwing it at his head. But I would get in *so* much trouble, so I squirrel it away in my pocket with my necklace.

My boredom has me looking around the room. Everyone is dressed so nicely – suits and dresses and shiny shoes. We look like the *new* New American families – some with plain skin, some with blue marks. I've noticed the marks on Jacks and Luxxe's moms look more feminine. They swirl, and the lines are daintier. They're beautiful.

I study my folded hands, thinking what they'd look like with the same type of marks, and I have a hard time imagining it. I then remember what Jacob said to me and Luxxe and Jacks before we left the building: "Let's all be on our best behavior today, okay?" We'd been cooped up for days on end, so he knew we were brimming with pent-up energy.

"Yes," my dad echoed. "Our race has already made spectacles of ourselves unintentionally. Today, the nation will see us on TV. Let's show them what good boys and girls we can be. How normal we are. We're like them."

A man opens the door, and we all straighten, waiting for him to invite us to leave. "The President would like to have a meeting with the Changer liaisons," he says, looking to our fathers.

Our fathers exchange confused looks, but the man gives no explanation. "Now, please, Mr. Foster," he insists, his steely eyes focusing on my dad.

They leave.

My boredom is near crippling at this point. If I never have to spend another minute in this stupid room, I wouldn't shed a tear. Our moms promise we'll go get ice cream after this as a reward. That's barely getting me through. *Barely.*

Spectacle

Noises outside the door snag my attention. It sounds like it's at the end of the hall. Shuffling feet. Muffled voices. The voices elevate, near shouting.

Our moms share concerned scowls.

One voice yells above the others. I don't recognize it. I think he says, "Get security!"

Security?

My mom starts for the door but thinks better of it. The other moms hover beside her.

We wait. Louder footsteps. Screaming voices. The terror seeping into my mom's face tells me something's wrong. She stoops over me now, wrapping me into her. She mouths to Luxxe's mom, but I can't see what. Luxxe's mom nods.

My heart pounds against my ribcage. Where's dad? I want to see my dad.

It's quiet now, and I take a minute to catch my breath. A noise shatters the silence. I can't even hear my own thoughts now as mom pulls me to the floor. I see her mouth open as she tries to scream, or maybe she's screaming but I can't hear.

The noise is pounding and intrusive. I don't like it. Fireworks? But it's inside, and it sounds like death and makes my skin bristle. My stomach lurches as I register what it is.

Gunfire.

The rest is a blur of terrified faces and clamor. Jacks' mom darting into the hallway. My mom reaching after her to stay. Something knocks her back into the room, red holes dotting her silk blouse.

Mom lays on me and covers my eyes. My world goes black.

Chapter 4

I must have passed out because I awake with a start, cradled in a strong man's arms. Not my dad. This man smells like oranges, his touch cold and unfeeling as he carries me down a hallway. "Mom," I croak out, my voice far-off. My ears buzz like mosquitos are living inside them.

The man says nothing.

I look for her but don't see her. I try and squirm free, but he holds me tighter. "Mom!" I cry. Where's my mom?

"Shhh," he says, more scolding than soothing, "You'll see her soon." I obey because he scares me. And because he wears a uniform like the others.

I notice we're not in the same building as before. The stark white walls, fluorescent lights, and bleach smell tell me we're in a hospital.

Spectacle

A nurse scurries by with a man on a stretcher and my anxiety swells. I want to wiggle again but I don't. A whimper escapes. Where are my parents? I want my parents....

The man takes me into a room where a doctor awaits. She sits on a stool beside a bed just big enough for someone my size. Her eyes roam over me with concern.

Why would I be hurt?

Gunfire, I remember, and my whimpering turns into a full-blown sob.

"She bleeding anywhere?" the doctor asks over my wailing.

He shakes his head, and with more care than I thought he was capable of, he places me on the bed beside her.

She waits for my cries to ebb and looks as though she wants to cradle me, but she doesn't.

"Where's... my mom..." I say between broken breaths.

Like the man, she doesn't give me an answer, though I can tell she's dying to.

Why won't she?

"Lie back," she soothes. Her red hair shines and is cut at an angle against her neck. Freckles splay across her nose, and there's kindness in her eyes.

I lie back as instructed and work on getting myself together. While her cold hands poke and prod, I stare at the ceiling, tears dripping onto the paper covering the bed. It crinkles as I relax under her touch.

I think of Jacks and Luxxe and their moms. Are they here too? Maybe when the doctor is done she'll let me see them.

Maybe everyone's okay.

After the doctor and man leave, I stay in the small room forever. It's been hours, I think, but I can't be sure since there's no clock. I keep hearing footsteps and murmurs in the hallway, but nobody comes to the door. Why isn't anyone coming for me?

Curled up in the fetal position, I fight my swollen eyelids. The blood in my veins runs thick and heavy, exhaustion weighing me down.

My eyelids flutter, but I force them open. I won't sleep until I see my parents again. I won't.

The buzzing lights above me flicker and I focus on a poster with some kind of medical chart across the room.

Stay awake.

The hallway is quiet now, and I curl into myself.

Within minutes, I'm out.

When I wake, the kind doctor is sitting next to me, a different uniformed man standing beside her. "Mirabella," she says, stroking my arm, "Wake up, dear. Some people need to talk to you." She says the words *some people* through her teeth and the pleasant look on her face wavers.

"Where are my parents?" I ask.

She sighs, looking defeated. I can't explain it, but she seems to have aged since I last saw her. Like she hasn't slept in days. "They're…" She searches for the words.

"You'll see them soon," the man says.

The doctor flashes him a look of menacing annoyance, then looks back to me, her features softening. "I know this is hard," she says. "But once you talk to them, we'll be able to discharge you."

"Discharge?"

"Let you go home," she clarifies.

I nod. Fine. Let's get this over with.

They lead me down a hallway to a dimly lit room. Only a rectangle table with two chairs, one on each side, occupies the center. A window sprawls across the wall separating this room from another. Through the window, I see the doctor take her place beside more men and women I've never seen. She looks even more displeased. I'm guessing she doesn't like what's about to happen.

I nervously fidget with the pearls around my neck.

Spectacle

The uniformed man helps me into one of the chairs. "Wait here," he says. "It will just be a moment."

Tentatively, I do as he says. If I do this, they'll let me go home. Nothing sounds better.

Within minutes, two men walk in, also in uniform, and one stays by the door while the other takes his seat across from me. His bronzed skin makes his soft green eyes almost glow, and the scar running along his left cheek would scare me if he didn't look at me with such pity. "Mirabella, right?" he says, scooting his chair closer to the table. The medals pinned to his uniform clink together.

"Yes," I manage. My voice sounds so small in this room with these unfamiliar men, and I feel swallowed whole, like I'm sitting in the belly of a whale. Vulnerable and uneasy.

He fights a frown and then forces it into a reassuring smile, the skin crinkling beside his eyes. "Lovely name," he says, and I can tell he means it. He looks at me the way a parent would do, full of compassion and worry, and I wonder if he has kids of his own.

Clearing his throat, he pulls a little black box from his pant pocket and sets it on the table. He pushes a button and a red light on top blinks to life. "This is a recorder," he explains. "That's all."

I give a short nod and reach for the chameleon pendant in my pocket. I rub my thumb over the ridge of its back.

After a quick glance at the people behind the window, he folds his hands on the table and begins. "Tell me what happened today, Mirabella." He pauses thoughtfully. "Is that what you like to be called?"

"Most people call me Mira," I say. "Except my mom." My voice breaks on *mom*. I ache to see her, to have her arms around me. Tears prick my eyes, but I swallow hard to help keep them where they are.

The man sighs as he watches me struggle, flashes another look through the window. A disapproving one this time. Like the doctor, he must not approve of what these people want from me but was probably given orders to do it anyway.

His gaze moves back to me. "I'll call you Mira, then," he says. "I like that."

"Okay."

"And you can call me Mr. K."

I think I nod.

"So, tell me what happened today," he repeats. "The first thing you remember."

"I..." What *do* I remember? Today feels a week long. "We came here in a taxi."

"Good," he says. "And then?"

"We were searched a lot by men in uniforms."

He pauses but remains stone-faced. Something about that threw him off. "Okay, good. And when you got here, what happened?"

"We went up an elevator and waited a long time in a room. Then a man came in and said the President wanted to meet with our dads."

He reclines in his chair, running a hand through his buzzed hair. I imagine it's stiff and itchy like dad's stubble. "And did your dad tell you why you were visiting the capitol today?"

This question confuses me. I thought everyone knew why we were visiting. "Because we were going to join him on TV." My reply comes out more like a question.

Mr. K's lips press tight, his eyes drawing to the window so quickly I'm not sure they noticed. His mouth opens to ask another question, but he thinks better of it. For some reason, my answer confuses him as much as his question did me.

He turns off the recorder and motions to the man at the door. "Thanks, Mira," he says, flashing one last smile, "You're free to go."

The man at the door escorts me out.

At the end of a long corridor, the man shows me to a room where Jacks and Luxxe sit in the middle. I cry out their names, which ends up sounding more like a gasp-sob, and they both look at me at the same time, their masks of bravery melting away. They too burst into tears as I hug them.

Spectacle

We sit like this for a good while - a huddle of interlocked bodies and sobs. After such a scary confusing day, it's nice to have some familiarity.

Once we're calm, we pull away and wipe our cheeks. They look a little embarrassed to have cried in front of each other. Boys are so weird.

"Where are our parents?" I ask. I find it odd they put us in here with no adults.

Luxxe shrugs and Jacks' face pinches in pain. He turns his head away and swipes at his cheeks. I then remember his mom and the bloody holes in her blouse. Did she make it? Does he even know if she did?

I don't ask, I only embrace him, and he cries silently into my shoulder. I cry along with him.

What a crappy, horrible day.

Jacks' Aunt Libby takes us home – well, to our apartment building – and the three of us settle in for the night at his place. Luckily, she gives us more information than the people at the hospital, but all she tells us is our parents are "being treated." And apparently, she agreed to take care of us until they're released. She also tells us it might be as long as a week before we see them again, but she refuses to talk about their conditions. Same with Luxxe's parents. Neither of us knows a thing.

When we left, news people waited for us outside, snapping our pictures from the building to the car. They kept shouting questions like "What happened this morning?" and "Have you seen the President? Is he okay?"

Aunt Libby told us to keep our heads down and not answer any questions.

I watch her now as she sneaks into a closet to make a phone call, so we won't hear. She appears dazed. Shattered. A lot like us. But she knows more and isn't saying. Sometimes I hate being a kid.

Jacks and Luxxe and I decide to sleep together on the living room floor. "Like a little camp-out," Aunt Libby says before she disappears with the phone. I give her brownie points for at least trying to *act* like everything is okay.

It's not, though. Something tells me after today, nothing will be the same.

"Night, Luxxe," I say, hugging a pillow against me.

"Night," he says.

"Night, Jacks."

He sniffles. "Night, guys."

Chapter 5

When they release mom a few days later, not in a week as we were told, she comes to get me. Of all our parents, she's the first to come home. After a tear-filled reunion, the first thing we do is check on the animals. Ryder and Trevor are in desperate need of food and water, but they are okay. The carpet in the living room is another story, thanks to Trevor. It'll take a while to get the smell out once we clean it. We didn't have an extra key for Aunt Libby to use to get in and tend to them.

Once we've cleaned up and taken showers, I find mom in the kitchen clutching a mug of green tea with one hand. Her other arm is in a sling hanging around her neck. She hunches over the mug at the table, the weight of everything bearing down on her. She looks frailer today, but not weaker, really. Not in the physical sense... except for her injured arm. She's hollowed out, a shell of herself. Like something's snuffed the light in her spirit.

"We need to talk, baby," she says, her glassy eyes meeting mine for a moment and then dragging back to her mug. Her free hand trembles as she smooths a strand of dark hair behind her ear.

I plant myself beside her and want to ask the obvious question – *where's dad?* – but I haven't been able to bring myself to mention him yet. I have a feeling she's a thread pull away from unraveling, and I want to tread lightly. I also don't know if I can handle the answer. If he were okay, wouldn't he be with us? I bite my lip to keep from crying.

Her hand moves to rest on mine, and after she closes her eyes and takes a long breath, she finally turns to face me. There's a glimmer of courage in her eyes. Not much, but it's there. "Mirabella," she says, her chin quivering.

Don't cry, mom. I'll lose it.

"Your father... and William and Jacob. They... they all..." Her teeth clench tight, her jaw straining to hold back a sob. A tear breaks free and travels along her cheek. "Oh, God," she chokes out, her hand meeting her forehead. Tears are dripping into her lap. She can't bear to finish.

I fling my arms around her neck and hold her, my own tears flowing fast and warm. She doesn't have to say it, and I don't want her to. If I hear the words, I'll die along with them.

When the sun buries itself behind the horizon and mom is fast asleep, I make my way up to the rooftop and sit in my usual place. I needed to escape our home and all the reminders of dad. Just a few days ago, he was sitting at the table with his morning coffee and breakfast. He was tickling me on the couch until I nearly threw up. He was scolding me for leaving my shoes on the living room floor where he could trip over them.

Despite my change in scenery, memories still find me here – how he marks... *marked*... every inch I grew on my door jamb. The way he

Spectacle

used to kiss me on my nose when he thought I was asleep but wasn't.

I choke on my tears, and then gasp for air, all of these things threatening to suffocate me. But really, losing him feels more like I imagine drowning to be - suspended in nothingness, a panic rising inside me, but despite my thrashing and crying, my fate is the same. My dad is gone. He's...

I sob into my hands.

My dad is gone.

Somehow, despite the burning, empty space in our hearts left by dad's death, mom and I manage to get up, get dressed and take care of ourselves and the animals every day. We don't leave the house, though. The news on the radio tells us how bad things are outside. Apparently, the humans have grown to fear the Changers. Even worse than before. Mom says it's loathing they feel, but fear and loathing are pretty much the same thing. I can't imagine why they'd feel either toward them, though. Changers aren't bad people. My gut tells me it's about what happened the day my father....

Because whenever a news report comes on that talks about the White House or mentions his name, she quickly turns it off. There's something she doesn't want me to hear. There's something she's protecting me from.

I hear her late at night when she thinks I'm sleeping. She yells at the radio that it's "all lies." And I can see it in her eyes, the anger. She gets mad all the time now and I fear it's destroying her. She's changed. Her eyes are harder, and she throws things. I'm afraid I won't recognize her one day because I'm already seeing sides to her that are unfamiliar. I guess sadness and rage, if allowed to fester, can turn someone into something they're not. I wish I knew how to help her, but I don't. We only have each other.

Hopefully, that's enough.

After dinner on a Sunday night, mom falls asleep on the couch while I play with Trevor on the floor. A light knock on the door arrests both our attention, and I clasp my hand around his muzzle before he has a chance to bark and wake mom.

"Mira!" a voice whispers through the door.

Jacks!

I run to the door and flatten myself against it, wishing I could open it and hug him tight. Mom keeps the key put up or I'd unlock it. "Hey, Jacks," I whisper back and glance at mom. Her eyelids flutter like they do when she's in a deep sleep. Hardly anything will wake her now.

"Mira!" he calls again. "You can't open the door? We need to talk…"

I know. We haven't seen each other since mom came and got me. "I can't. I don't know where the key is. Your mom home yet? Everything okay?"

Stupid question, I know. Nothing is *okay* anymore.

"She is. She's still in pain, though. They told her bullet wounds take a while to heal."

"Sorry, Jacks."

"S'okay."

"Is that what you came to tell me?"

"No… It's about our dads. You hear what they're saying on the news?"

My heart leaps into my throat, and my mouth goes dry. "No," I finally say. "Mom won't let me hear. What are they saying?"

"They're…" he hesitates. "You really don't know?"

"*No,*" I say a little too loudly. My heartbeat pulses behind my ears. "Tell me!"

"They're saying our dads started the gunfire at the White House. That they went there to attack the President."

I smother a gasp with my hand.

"It's not true, though," he adds. "They're lying."

My hand falls away and my knees are suddenly made of jelly. I wilt to the floor. "Obviously," I say, staring at the door in disbelief. Our dads don't own guns. I don't think. And we were only there for a… what did they call it? A press conference. "Why?" I ask.

Spectacle

"I don't know. But now everyone's saying we're dangerous and can't be trusted. They're calling what happened an act of war."

"But we're not," I say. "It wasn't."

"I know. But now that people think that, they're being mean to the Changers, and we're fighting back. And now they're calling *us* violent. It's not fair."

I reel, words failing me. How is this happening? *Why* is this happening? I look back to my mom again and realize her anger has been justified. Her husband, my father, was taken from us and labeled a criminal. As a man who started this war. No wonder our kind is feared and loathed. We're *dangerous*. But if our dads didn't start the gunfire that day, who did?

"You still there?" he asks. "I gotta get going before my mom realizes I'm gone."

"Yeah," I say weakly.

"It'll be okay," he says, but I know he can't really promise such a thing. But that's what we do, we protect each other. We stick together. "Tell your mom our families are planning to leave for the mountains tomorrow night. Others are talking about hiding out there and we plan on joining them. My mom said she's going to call yours in the morning."

"Okay," I say. "Bye, Jacks."

"Bye."

I lie in my bed and stare at the ceiling. Dad covered them with glow-in-the-dark stars for my tenth birthday. I think of leaving for the mountains and I'm filled with a mixture of agony and relief. In a way, I don't want to leave this place; memories of my father, as painful as they can be, are everywhere and it's all I have left of him now. But in another, I want to start fresh, even if we have to live in huts or caves or whatever they're planning on doing. The thought unnerves me a little, like any unknown thing, but it'll be good for mom to leave here and be around others. And I'll be able to see Jacks and Luxxe more; I desperately need their company.

A knock on the front door startles me. It was too loud to be Jacks or Luxxe. A man shouts through it, but I can't make out what he's saying from here. Trevor is going wild.

Mom stirs on the couch and I wait to see if she'll get it.

The man shouts again, and her feet patter my way. She finds me erect on the bed with my covers wrapped around me in a cocoon. Her eyes are huge white saucers, and she presses her finger against her lips to keep me quiet before she shuts my door and sprints away.

Alone in my room, I hide inside the space between my bed and the wall and snatch a book of Robert Frost poems on my nightstand, hugging it close for comfort. To distract myself, I try to recite *The Road Not Taken* but can't focus enough to do so. My heart gains speed as panic courses through me. Whoever is on the other side of the door has her worried. Are we in danger? I've never wanted my dad more than I do in this moment. This isn't right. He should be here to protect us. If I wasn't so scared, I'd pay more attention to the anger writhing inside me. I hope whoever took him from us is dead. I hope they're gone for what they did.

The man shouts louder this time and bangs three times on the door. I still hear Trevor, but where's mom? I don't hear mom!

After an eternity, she shows up again with a bag slung over her shoulder and points to my cracked window. She wants to escape. But where would we go? I nod silently and stand, slipping the book into my waistband.

A loud bang rattles our apartment, and the living room door hurls into the kitchen. Splinters of wood lie in its wake. In one swift movement, mom snatches me by the arm and heaves the window open the rest of the way.

The thumping of loud boots fills our apartment, and to keep from screaming out, I bite my tongue so hard it bleeds. The men in uniforms, they're here for us.

She helps me halfway through the window, and my foot barely touches the cold metal platform of the fire escape when she's ripped away from me. Men wrestle her to the ground as though her kicking and thrashing are no stronger than a newborn baby's. I reach out for her, crying her name.

Spectacle

"Go, Mira!" she wails. "Get out of here."

As the men pin her against a wall, another one just makes it through my door. Trevor is clamped to his pant leg and shaking it furiously, but he kicks him away. I scream as I watch him fly and hit the wall. Trevor tries to stumble to his feet and then passes out. "Get the girl!" one of the other men shouts.

"Mira!" mom screams. "*Go.*"

I hesitate as he starts for me, everything within me wanting to help my mom and Trevor, but I know I can't. I can't leave them, either. I can't.

My mom is sobbing my name now, and I go willingly as the man snatches me back into the room. If we're being taken away by these men, at least it will be together. We have to stay together. Dad would want it that way.

The man takes me in his arms and hugs me tight in case I try to struggle, but I don't. "Take her away," another man in the living room orders. He stands there watchful, appraising. He must be in charge.

I register that he said "her", not "them", and I throw my mom a desperate look as the man heads with me for the living room. She's struggling harder now, letting out a string of strangled cries, what little good it's doing her. My numbing fear gives way to anger, and I struggle too, wiggling an arm free. They're not taking me from her!

I claw at the man's face with all I have, hoping he'll drop me, and he stumbles, blood dribbling down his forehead. Once he regains his footing, he crushes me into him and I can't breathe. "Little bitch," he mumbles.

The man in charge slaps me as we pass, white-hot pain splintering across my cheek. The room and mom's cries swirl around me. I hear a gunshot.

She goes silent.

"See? Even the little ones are animals," the man in charge spits out. "Now take her to the shuttle. Unit 1B is next."

Chapter 6

About once a month I have a recurring nightmare, except technically, it isn't a nightmare; it's vivid, painful memories haunting me while I sleep – the man in the uniform carrying me out to a bus filled with other Changers and their kids; Jacks and I huddled together with his mom and Aunt Libby while Luxxe cries into his mom's shoulder; crippling fear consuming us as we wonder where they're taking us and what will happen once we get there.

That was six years ago.

Once I wake from these nightmares, usually covered in sweat and clutching my chameleon pendant, I know how the rest of it goes: they herd us like cattle into government ships and take us to an island far off the coast. An island nobody knew existed... not the citizens of New America, anyway. Not until the government wanted to use it.

Spectacle

They dumped us here with minimal provisions, if you want to call them that, to fend for ourselves. It was better than a straight execution, but not really. How did they know we wouldn't die from starvation or disease? I suppose they didn't care. Good thing we're survivalists by nature. We adapt. And at least here, while there's still the threat of wild boar and mountain lions and rattlesnakes, our chances are better than living with the humans who feared and hated us.

Not by much, though.

This morning, in what I'm guessing is late August, as the sun slips through the space between the linen covering my window and the wall, I sit up to peel off my sweat-covered shirt and assess how sore I am. I was up until midnight last night with Luxxe, so he could give me spear-throwing lessons before our monthly hunt this evening.

Ugh.

I'd rather relive my nightmares ten times over than hunt. I'd rather do *anything* than hunt. Stupid tribal traditions. If I didn't care about disrespecting the Elders, I'd refuse to go.

As I weave my hair into a long braid, Jacks' voice croaks from the next room. "Mira." Our hand-built home, made of logs and mud with layers of reeds for the roof, is just big enough for the two of us. His mom adopted me when we arrived, and Jacks and I used to share a room. When she passed from a snake bite two years ago, I moved into her room to give us more privacy. Now I'm the one overseeing his care. He's my family now. Other than Luxxe and his mom, Jacks is all I have left.

"Coming," I reply, stretching as I stand. Yep, the muscles in my right shoulder and torso are *killing*.

I change into a black tank top and jeans, lace up my worn leather boots and shuffle my way to the next room. "A little help, please?" he says with his usual cheery grin. His light brown eyes, puffy from sleep, shine at me through his glasses. A hairline crack zigzags across the right lens. "I need to, uh…"

Right. Bathroom.

"You act like you're helpless or something," I tease, and loop his arm around my neck. We both know he is helpless but joking keeps us from mourning over it. Grimacing inwardly, I try to ignore the aching in my sides as I pull him to his feet.

"I know," he replies, and I help him hobble toward our front and only door. His feet turn inward now, his weakened legs a shell of what they used to be. "I just like being waited on."

I lightly nudge him with my elbow. "Ya big faker."

We make it outside, and the air is thick with morning dew. The pine trees and maples encircling our little shack-of-a-cabin swallow it whole but provide a good bit of shade. Soon, when the sun climbs higher, the humidity will be nearly unbearable. Shade is everything this time of year.

After helping Jacks with his cotton shorts, he leans against a tree to do his business. I turn my head away and try to think of something else. Anything else. The birds above us sing a cheery song, and I look to my garden and notice some of my peppers have ripened and are ready to be picked. Among the provisions the government oh so graciously left us, they included a week's worth of perishables. Tabitha, Jacks' mom, had a knack for making things grow, so we collected seeds from what vegetables we could and started a garden.

We miss her more than words can say but thinking of how proud she'd be that I kept her garden flourishing, I smile a little. But really, I'm the one who's grateful. Because of her, I have an outlet. Growing and tending to things helps me not feel so dead inside. It gives me purpose. When they first left us here, I thought I'd never recover from the pain, which eventually became an all-consuming numbness. Luxxe's mom said it was so I could cope. Caring for Jacks and our little home here keeps me going. It's helped me feel again.

Once I get him fed and settled back inside, I'll get to work before Luxxe comes to steal me away for the afternoon. He wants to practice more before tonight.

My smile wavers.

Spectacle

Two bucketsful later, I'm ready to take my harvest to the creek for a good wash before I have to leave. The sun is almost directly overhead. He'll be here soon.

I down a gulp of water from my jug and stand, wiping the sweat from my brow with the back of my hand. My knees are stiff: I'd knelt for too long, so I squat a few times to loosen them. At least my sore muscles have eased some.

And then I hear it: that high-pitched, breathy voice. "Bella!"

Nolie. A girl who lives with her mom in a cabin down the path. The only person who calls me by a different nickname.

I sigh and talk myself into being patient with her. Had I not spent time in the garden, I wouldn't be in the mood. As funny as she can be sometimes, unknowingly so, I have to take her in doses. I also have to remind myself she's younger and I'm probably her only friend. We're the only ones in our tribe who choose not to live amongst the others in huts. Me, because I need more space to help with Jacks, and her... well, her mom is a bit of a handful.

I guess you could say we live in the *special needs* wing of camp.

"Bella!" she yells again and skids to a stop behind me. I turn to offer her a drink but bark out a laugh instead. My hand slaps over my mouth. I couldn't control it.

"What?" she asks, but her wounded expression tells me she knows.

"What happened to your... um..." It looks as though a deranged monkey got ahold of her hair.

She purses her lips, her gaze falling to the ground between us. "Mom," she mumbles. "She cut it. Thought it was too long."

Correction. It looks like a mentally unstable parent with a drinking problem got ahold of it. I give her a strained, sympathetic smile. "Yeesh... sorry, Noles." I contemplate telling her it doesn't look that bad, but I can't will myself to lie. I already laughed at her. Poor thing. And she has such pretty hair too – that typical Changer dark brown.

In a futile attempt to make it look better, she smooths her hand over her jagged bangs. "Hey," she says, taking note of my full buckets, "Need help with that?"

"I'm good, thanks." I'm a bit selfish when it comes to my gardening. It's the only thing I have that's solely mine. "So, what's new?" I ask and glance down the path. Suddenly, I want Luxxe to be here sooner than later.

"Was actually going to see if you remembered where we put the rabbit snares. I couldn't find them this morning."

My eyes trail down to a limp rabbit in her hand. "Um… you have one in your hand, Nolie."

"Oh, yeah… this," she says, giving it a gentle shake. Its head and legs jiggle like a rag doll's. "I could only find one."

I want to roll my eyes so bad I can't stand it. I've only shown her where the traps are five times. Sometimes I think she uses it as an excuse to spend time with me, but as she peers up at me under her jagged fringe of bangs, her brown doe eyes pleading, I cave, as always. Besides, I know what it's like to have to care for someone day in and day out. You need a break. "Let me tell Jacks I'm leaving."

Luxxe can wait. It won't kill him.

Chapter 7

Our snares caught a raccoon and three rabbits, one of which Nolie's mom let me have. She said she didn't like the way its "eyes looked" ... whatever that means. That was before she mumbled about leprechauns and passed out against their door frame. Nolie and I *assumed* that meant I could have it, anyway. So, I'm taking it home to make a stew for dinner.

When I arrive, Luxxe is leaning against the large oak in our front yard with an impatient scowl. God forbid he has to wait on me. Or anyone. "You know your face is gonna stick like that," I say, unintimidated by his grouchiness. I'm probably the only person our age here who isn't intimidated by him in one form or another. But then again, I remember he used to sleep on Batman sheets and liked his mom to rub his back, so he could fall asleep. Kind of shatters the whole tough, hunter-man persona.

And when I say man, he really does look like a man at a frightening seven feet tall, muscles rolling and rippling down his back and chest and arms. He wears his hair in the traditional Changer dreadlocks and nothing but a pair of shorts made from the hide of whatever animal he killed.

Once we settled on the island, the Elders encouraged us to adopt their old traditions, which most of the Changers gladly accepted. Including Luxxe, obviously. I prefer a more human look and way of living, so luckily for me, everyone donated their 'human' clothes to me and Jacks so they could traipse around in their animal skins. In a way, I find it silly to deny my human heritage. Besides, my thin, light hair would look ridiculous in dreads; I'd look like I'm trying too hard to fit in. I also don't have any markings yet. Neither does Jacks. Since I'm three months shy of seventeen, every morning I expect Jacks to tell me some have formed at the corners of my eyes — the place they usually start. Jacks has been waiting for the same. Luxxe's are already cascading down his neck and covering his broad, tan shoulders. Although I don't have the hots for him, *at all*, I can see why most girls in our tribe do. He's pretty dang attractive… for a turd muncher.

I hang the dead rabbit over a low-lying branch beside him and punch his shoulder for still scowling. His muscle barely gives. "I said your face is gonna stick!"

"I heard you," he says, and the corner of his mouth twitches with a smirk. He can't stay mad at me for long. "How's Jacks?"

I shrug but manage a hopeful smile. "He's Jacks. Woke up cheerful as always." I jab him again. "You could learn a thing or two from him."

Luxxe jabs me back but gentler. "Maybe if I didn't spend half my life waiting around for you, I'd be a little more cheerful. You're always late."

I roll my eyes. "Only for the things I'm not excited about." Like barbaric hunting expeditions.

"I know, I know," he says, tugging my braid. I smile wider. I love how we can be ourselves when nobody else is around. And nobody

Spectacle

meaning his girlfriend, Taylor. She'd have a coronary if she knew we were... *gasp*... alone and touching each other. Even in a friendly way.

She's ridiculous.

But he loves her, and so I try to keep my attitude toward her respectful. Outwardly, anyway. My thoughts are my own; I can think whatever I want.

My face falls at the thought of her.

Luxxe sighs. "You really have no interest in practicing again, do you?"

I shake my head with a dramatic pout. He doesn't have to know my lack of enthusiasm is mostly because I'm thinking of Taylor, but no, I also have no interest in practicing, either. My muscles can't take any more spear-chucking.

"You know you could get hurt tonight if we don't," he says. "The better prepared you are-"

"The safer I'll be," I finish for him. I've only heard this lecture a million times.

He chuckles, his massive shoulders bouncing. "Fine," he concedes, almost grunts. "Whatcha need help with around here? Mom will be here later to help with Jacks."

I look at the rabbit pointedly.

"Let me guess," he says, shaking his head in mock disappointment, "You want me to clean it for you?"

I give him a sheepish grin. "Pretty please?" Cleaning animals is *not* my thing. Blech.

"I wonder about you, Mira," he says, slinging the rabbit over his shoulder and heading for the cabin to get a knife, "I doubt you have any Changer in you at all."

Something else I've heard him say a million times, but I often wonder the same.

The sun hides behind the treetops, wild rays of light fighting their way through the branches and pouring in through the front door. I

love this time of day – the promise of cooler air and singing insects to come.

After dinner, I usually sit with Jacks until he falls asleep, then make my way outside and wait with the serenading insects for the stars to greet us. Like gardening and the stars, it centers me. It makes me whole.

Too bad I won't be back until dark.

I peek through my window, and Luxxe's mom, Maggie, hovers over the rabbit stew outside while Luxxe entertains Jacks with another one of his hunting stories. She tears at some herbs and sprinkles them in, the rich peppery fragrance wafting my way. I suck in a lungful and my mouth waters. Almost ready.

Sensing my eyes on her, Maggie shoots me a kind, maternal smile and then turns her attention to the boys, her beaded necklaces and bracelets clattering together. Six years ago, she looked like a different woman. She wore her hair in a bob and always had on jeans with collared shirts and pearls. I thought of her as elegant and well put together. And in a way, despite her dreads and animal hide dress and strings of wooden jewelry, she still is. It's the way she has about her – always graceful, always caring and pleasant. Luxxe could learn some things from her too. He has more of his dad in him, I guess.

After dinner, Maggie sits with Jacks on his mat and works on one of her baskets. Everyone here has taken up a trade, so they can barter for things they need, like me with my vegetables. I remind myself to slip her a few extra cucumbers for helping with Jacks tonight. Those are her favorite.

"Ready to go?" Luxxe asks. He has to bend slightly to peer through the front door. I'm guessing by his panting and the sheen of sweat on his brow he was exercising while Maggie and I cleaned up after dinner. Always staying in shape. Always preparing for the next hunt.

I turn back to what I was doing and act like I didn't hear him, humming to myself and drying an already dry wooden bowl before I put it away. "Mira…" he says. "It's time."

Spectacle

I pretend to scrape at a piece of food stuck to the side of it. Fighting a smirk, I look to Maggie. "So, tell me again, what is it you weave those baskets with?"

She fights a smirk of her own. "Oh, ya know..." she says, cutting her eyes at her son for a fraction of a second, "...sometimes I use reeds. Sometimes strips of cane."

"Interesting," I say, returning the bowl to its home on a shelf above our washtub.

To get my attention, a rock whistles by my ear and ricochets off the wall. I swallow a bout of giggles and continue. "Maybe you could teach me how to do that sometime, Maggie. I just *love* your baskets." I'm so mean. His blood *has* to be boiling.

Her voice strains to keep her own laughter at bay. "Sure, dear."

Luxxe grunts, and then says through his teeth, "Mira, I swear you're gonna get it if you don't come on!"

Idle threats. *So* scary. Although he does give a mean headlock-knuckle sandwich combo. Maybe I better....

His large feet trudge my way, and I squeal. The humored annoyance in his eyes tells me he's more playful than angry. I hold up my arms in surrender, but he hoists me over his shoulder anyway. I lie there defeated as he carries me out. "Bye, guys!" he says, ducking under the door frame.

I wave my goodbyes to Maggie and Jacks, who're both laughing at us, but Jacks' expression holds a tinge of concern. I know he worries on hunting day. Even though I'm with Luxxe he fears I might get hurt. "See you in no time!" I assure him – the thing I tell him every time I leave – and, as always, he puts on a mask of bravery and smiles wider.

Chapter 8

I focus on keeping up with Luxxe's long strides as we walk beside each other, the ferns reaching for the center of the path and brushing against my jeans. It annoys me more than usual. Probably because we're close to camp and Luxxe has hardly said a word. It's at least a twenty-minute walk, and all the times before he talked my ear off about the happenings there – which one of his friends killed the most boars or deer that week; whose relationships ended and whose had started; who's sick; who's better. Anything and everything. I feel like I know most of them well, though none of them really know me... except for the ones I barter with. This time, Luxxe mostly stares at the ground in deep thought, his thick eyebrows drawn together.

"Okay, what's going on?" I blurt out. "What happened between the house and now that as you all clammed up?"

He shrugs.

Spectacle

"Luxxe," I demand, grabbing his arm. He stops, but not because I'm strong enough to make him. "Is it because we didn't practice today?"

His eyes slowly drag up to mine. Beneath them lies something dark and almost sad, but he tries to smile it away. This is way deeper than his usual grumpy mood. This is crucial. "I'm fine," he says and presses his full lips tight.

I give him a "yeah, right" look.

He scans the trees around us and looks as though he wants to tell me but doesn't. That confirms it. For whatever reason, he's keeping something from me. "Let's go," he mumbles. "I'm sure they're waiting on us."

Borderline exasperated, I watch as he ignores my pleading look and lumbers on his way. I follow silently after him. He'll tell me when he's ready.

He better.

We thread through the empty market at the fringes of camp. Mornings through early afternoons it teems with tribesmen, those selling goods and those bartering. These long strings of tables are where I trade peppers with Deidre for her natural soaps, or squash and potatoes with Mr. Fritz when we have a hankering for goat cheese or apples. I try to only come once every two weeks, so I don't have to leave Jacks by himself more than necessary.

Trying to keep my thoughts off whatever is bothering Luxxe, I focus on the smoke in the distance billowing into a vibrant pink and orange sky. *Almost there.* My heart skips a beat and then drops, a mixture of anxiety and dread filling me. We're moments away from hunting. It happens once a month, and all tribesmen – hunters by trade or not – are asked to participate if they're over sixteen and physically capable (which, for me, is debatable) but it's to encourage togetherness. It's Changer tradition. And whatever we kill tonight is skinned and prepared for a feast tomorrow night. Now *that* I don't mind so much. I can eat my weight in deer meat.

When the tables end, we walk down a narrow path that spits us out into a clearing with the charred remains of a bonfire in the middle. Changers congregate at the far end near the wood line, and I pause, staring timidly into the milling cluster of leather-hide clothes and blue markings. Everyone holds handmade spears or axes or bows and quivers, and some are already yelping out battle cries. Every time I come to these things I'm out of my element. I'd rather be at home in the calm comfort of the stars and garden and my sweet, freckled friend.

Luxxe stops with me, placing a supportive hand on my shoulder. I glance up at him, and the sadness in his eyes is gone. He must have come back from whatever grave place he was living in. The promise of a new kill, I'm sure. "Just stick by me," he says, pulling me into his side and ushering me toward the crowd.

As always, my thoughts echo. Sometimes I wonder if he thinks of me as a hindrance on these nights, though he never lets on if he does.

Before we're swallowed whole by the sea of Changers, I scan their living quarters along the creek to the east. Sprinkled beside it in no specific pattern are huts made of sticks and mud and waxy leaves. What few aging tribesmen we have are huddled around small fires with blankets wrapped around their shoulders, their wrinkled skin altering the blue patterns on their cheeks. Our tribal Elders, Blythe and Jonah, along with the fourteen and fifteen-year-olds, tend to the kids near the riverbank to keep them occupied while their parents are away. Some of them are building sandcastles. Some of them run around squealing and chasing butterflies.

Despite the war cries ahead, everything here appears so stable and calm. Like this is the way it's always been. Like we weren't dumped here to fend for ourselves six years ago. Of course, this place will turn on us if we drop our guard for too long; it isn't without its dangers. Tabitha could attest to that.

I often wonder, though, when I'm here at camp amongst the beautiful chaos, if the ones with human ties (ex-friendships and lovers, coworkers, adoptive families) have forgotten that part of their history. Or perhaps, they're burying themselves in this new way of life to help them forget so they don't have to hurt over it, though I don't judge them if they are. I do my fair share of burying things as well. Maybe it's because I'm the only one in our tribe who's half human, who has an actual blood tie to the human race, but it would feel like a lie for me to deny that part of myself and only claim the other. I suppose, in one form or another, whether we bury or remember, we're all trying to carry on and make the best of it. What else can we do?

When Luxxe and I make it into the crowd, they part for us, their cheers and attentions trained on Luxxe – the camp's hunting trainer and star of said hunts. In other words, their well-respected, sometimes feared, hero. I've seen him hunt enough to know why too. He's precise and brutal. No holds barred. It's safe to say he's the best one here, and I have to admit, though anything violent makes my stomach turn - even for the purpose of food - to see him in his element is like witnessing the athleticism of an Olympian god. This is what he was made for – to kill.

His arm slips from my shoulder as he turns to hug his best friend and training assistant, Cole - another mountain of a teenage boy. He wears his dreads shorter, and his eyes are the color of liquid metal. His markings have harsh angles like bolts of lightning and cover his arms and half his torso. They've multiplied since I last saw him.

The cheers around us ebb as they wait for Luxxe to finish his greetings and lead us into the forest; this is the part where I have to fend for myself. Then we'll part ways into smaller groups and kill whatever we can carry. Our group is usually me, Luxxe, Taylor, and Cole.

While I stand with my hands clasped and looking at the ground, the lonely snowflake in a frenzied bed of coal, I feel some of their eyes on me but pretend not to notice. I know they wonder about me – the blonde, pale girl with no markings who hardly ever comes around; the girl Luxxe is close with even though he has a very committed girlfriend, not that it's any of their business; the daughter of the former head liaison who met with the President all those years ago. Though most believe my dad is innocent, I think some blame him for starting the war that placed us here, though they don't say it.

At least not to me. I've overheard rumblings in the market a time or two about how he went *mad* or *rogue* and secretly planned to take the President out but was taken out instead. And it might be my imagination, but I feel their resentment when they look at me, still fresh after all this time. Like I was somehow in on whatever they assume he did.

Oh, well. Screw them. He was innocent.

"Hey, Mira," Cole says, turning his attention to me as Luxxe makes his way to the front of the crowd. In a lot of ways, I'm coming to think of him as my third brother. He's good at rescuing me from my awkward loneliness when Luxxe has other things to do. Here, it's easy for me to feel alone in a crowd. And impossibly short.

He gives me a friendly side-hug, and I although I want to shrink into the space between his arm and ribcage until we head out, I resist the urge and pull my shoulders back to fake some confidence.

"Hey," I say back.

His eyes twinkle with bloodlust like Luxxe's. "You ready?"

"As I'll ever be."

"Atta girl."

Luxxe's voice carries over the chatter around us, silencing it. "Can I get everyone's attention?" Beside him stands Taylor in all her striking glory – cerulean eyes to match her markings, olive skin and a mouthful of perfect white teeth. She likes to wear the height of teenage Changer fashion, her hide crop-top and shorts exposing more of her skin than necessary, a cluster of feathers dangling from her dreads. Jonah is her uncle, and by the regal way she carries herself, you can tell she's proud of it. And of her relationship with Luxxe.

She damn well better be proud of that.

Luxxe then gives his routine lecture about everyone staying in groups and making sure they at least have one weapon on them. They're not only for hunting, they're for self-defense if we happen upon a disgruntled hog or rattler.

Crap. Forgot my machete.

I feel a tug on my waist, and I look down to see Cole's hands belting his machete around me. "Cole!" I hiss. "Keep it. It's yours."

Spectacle

"You need it more than me," he insists, cinching the belt snugly around my hips before turning and pretending to listen to Luxxe again.

"*Cole*," I whisper, seething. My fingers fumble with the knot he tied but I can't work it loose. I'd never forgive myself if he needs his machete and gets hurt because he gave it to me.

He ignores me, and I can tell by the way his cheek twitches that he's smirking. This isn't *remotely* funny. "*Cole*... Take it back."

Changers around us are staring now, but I don't care. Cole doesn't either because his shoulders bounce with a chuckle. He's as infuriating as Luxxe sometimes.

"Fine," I grumble, and I know what Luxxe would tell me – "Just let someone take care of *you* for once." That infuriates me too, though I know he's right. I have a hard time accepting help. Being without my parents for so long has made me that way – annoyingly independent.

Changers burst into cheers around me, and I jump. Luxxe must have ended his speech and given a final inspiring word. Thanks to Cole, I haven't been paying attention.

"And stay safe out there!" Luxxe adds as the crowd disperses.

My irritation gives way to unease, and I swallow over the lump in my throat. *Great... it's time.*

Chapter 9

I always stay in the back of our four-man hunting team.

Mostly because I'm an inexperienced hunter, but also because my footfalls aren't as quiet, and I don't want to scare away anything they might want to kill. It annoys Luxxe to no end that I wear shoes, especially to hunt in, but it's the smarter choice around here. I may be louder, but I'm better protected.

You can ask Tabitha about that as well. And Jacks' Aunt Libby. A rattlesnake got her while she was out looking for berries our first summer here.

As we slink through the woods – shoulders hunched, breathing carefully, eyes roaming for prey and dangers – I silently hope for a deer or hog to present itself, so we can get this over with. It's the perfect time of day to see one: the sun is on the verge of setting completely. The woods are calm and cool. Animals are on the move.

Spectacle

This part of the hunt I don't mind – before the rush of adrenaline and violence.

As if Luxxe heard my hopes for a quick hunt and wants to grant it, he crouches lower and stiffens, the muscles across his shoulders tightening. My heartbeat quickens.

He's spotted something.

Moving like apparitions, Taylor and Cole quickly and silently sidle up to him and search for whatever alerted him. Taylor goes rigid, then Cole. I can't see what they've spotted thanks to a cluster of wiry pine trees, so I steady my breathing and lean against a nearby maple until this is over. They'll sit like this awhile until they get a good shot.

Moments pass, and they haven't moved. They must be close to striking, though, because the color of Luxxe's skin morphs darker to match the earth. Green streaks up his side and races across his back to camouflage him with the surrounding ferns. Taylor and Cole follow suit, and if I were to blink and look away, I'd lose them.

These moments always remind me of Ryder, the way he could will his skin color to change, and I ignore the aching in my heart. I don't allow myself to mourn for the things I was forced to leave behind. What good would it do?

A rustling behind me snags my attention, but I remain still and keep my eyes on Luxxe. Probably a squirrel or lizard. The rustling approaches and then seemingly multiplies. I hear snorts and grunts.

Hogs.

My hand itches for my machete, not to purposefully kill one, but out of instinct, in case one charges. Hogs typically run away, but my luck, I would spook one or piss it off in some way and it would come charging. And if one is a boar, his tusks would shred my legs into ground meat.

Ever so slowly, I turn my head, and I'm relieved to see they're piglets. Two months old, tops. They're rooting around in the brush a couple yards to my left. My mouth quirks into a smile as I watch them, but it doesn't take long for me to piece together what Luxxe is waiting to kill – their mom. A sow.

My stomach sinks. *No...*

I debate calling ahead to my hunting partners. Since we consider hogs to be nuisance animals, it's not against our rules to kill a sow when their young are with them, but it's against everything within me to let it happen. The most vulnerable fibers of my being, woven throughout the raw and hidden places of my soul, are crying out to prevent this. It's not right.

I know what it's like to lose a parent.

"Luxxe," I whisper, my eyes searching frantically for the subtle curves of his outline. I've already lost him. "*Luxxe.*"

"Shhh," I hear, a faint, scornful warning as light as a breeze, and I follow it to find Taylor's blue eyes boring into me – hard, sapphire jewels set in the earth-tone camouflage of her skin. I ignore her look of disdain and point to the piglets. Her eyes immediately soften, and she nudges Luxxe. There... I see him again.

In a move so soft I barely register it, he turns his head and eyes the piglets... for all the good it does. He rolls his dark eyes as if he's irritated we bothered to alert him. To cause him to move and risk a potential kill.

Jerk. Should have known he wouldn't care. I know Taylor feels the same as me, but she won't do anything about it. And Cole will only follow Luxxe's lead. He's no help, either.

Guess it's up to me.

So be it.

"Let's keep going," I say, making a point to say it loud enough to spook the hogs close to us but not all the animals in the forest.

Luxxe shoots me a look that could kill, and I hear the babies behind me scatter. I cross my arms defiantly. I *dare* him to scold me.

Something behind him makes a horrible grunting sound, following by clacking and gnashing of teeth.

Shit. It's a boar, not a sow.

Tusks.

Luxxe catapults to his feet, poising his spear to strike in self-defense, but the boar dashes off in a blur of chestnut-colored hair and squeals.

Good... He bailed.

Spectacle

They drop their camoflauge, so no one accidentally hurts the other with a weapon.

"I've got it!" Cole yells, shoving an arrow into his bow and drawing back. He pivots to match the boar's stride, one eye squinted, the other trained on his target. For whatever reason, my father's face flashes through my mind.

"No!" I yell.

My panicked voice makes him jump, and he releases the arrow prematurely; it goes sailing through the forest, never to be seen again. His jaw flexes with anger, his cheeks burning red.

Taylor glares at me. *"Seriously?"*

The object of their disapproving scowls, I stand there alone, justified in my actions but much hated. I muster a look of confidence. I did the right thing.

"Mira…" Luxxe scolds.

I don't know why, but tears surface. I feel silly and angered that they show up in this moment, but I can't make them leave. I couldn't let them kill that boar. I couldn't let a father be taken from its young. I couldn't. I couldn't.

A tear rolls down my cheek, but I ignore it. I cross my arms tighter – to both show continued defiance and soothe myself.

The hard lines of Luxxe's scowl melt into a frown. If *I'm* crying, he knows something's wrong. He drops his spear and heads for me. I want to back away from him, I'm still mad at him, but I let him come.

Three strides in, he freezes, his eyes shifting to the side. The dread seeping into his face makes my heart skip. I manage to say: "What is-"

"Cole," he says, interrupting me. His voice is low and cautious. "Toss me my spear. You're the closest to it."

That's when I hear it – a hoof digging at the earth. Grunts. Clacking. The blood drains from my cheeks. *It's back.*

"Dude…" Cole says. "As soon as I reach for it, he'll charge."

"I don't have time to argue, man. Just do it."

"I can get it with my bow," he counters.

Taylor interjects. "Give him the spear, Cole!"

The boar grunts some more, moving closer, challenging us.

I think about reaching for my machete, but wait, standing as stone still as possible. Luxxe will tell me what I need to do. "Someone do *something*," I whimper.

"Oh, so *now* you want us to kill it?" Taylor snaps.

I hope she can feel the daggers I'm shooting her.

"Knock it off, you two," Luxxe says. "Cole... *spear!*"

As Cole moves to do it as smoothly as possible, Luxxe fixes his attention on me. "Whatever you do, Mira, don't run, okay? He's faster than you. He'll catch you."

My mouth goes dry. "He wants *me?*"

"I think so... you were closer to the babies."

Or the easier-looking target.

"But did you hear me? Don't run."

I nod, I think. I can't get hurt. I can't. Jacks needs me...

Another tear rolls along my cheek, then another. Why can't I have my marks yet? Then I'd be able to camouflage myself.

When Cole tosses the spear to Luxxe, it excites the boar, and he charges. A scream rips up my throat unbidden, and I instinctively skitter in the other direction. I ram into a tree, knocking the air from my lungs.

"Mira!" Luxxe cries. "Be still..."

The boar charges faster — all two-hundred pounds of muscle, bristling fur and wild eyes. "Luxxe," I choke out.

Luxxe launches into motion, leaping into the air so the boar will pass under him, his spear poised above his head. I watch the charging boar and Luxxe in all his athletic glory, and everything moves in slow motion. My chest tingles, the place where my frantic heart hammers against my breastbone and moves in waves to my limbs. I'm out of body. Disconnected.

I'm panicking.

I try to cry out, but my throat pinches tight. I can't say anything at all. All I can focus on is the boar. His eyes. More death and hate lay there than I've ever seen. He wants me gone. He's coming for me.

The tingles envelop me and mutate into a paralyzing heat. It's scalding and shredding my insides.

Wait...

Spectacle

This is more than panic. But what? I can't think. I just want to scream in pain, but it's useless. I need to get away. Away from here. Even if it's a few yards. But I can't move.

Blackness lingers at the fringes of my vision and creeps slowly inward. I'm losing my grip. I'm passing out. Crap... *I'm passing out!*

The last thing I see is Luxxe's spear plunging into the hog's side, and then all sights and sounds and excruciating pains are lost to the dark.

I'm gone.

Chapter 10

"How did she get here?" a voice asks – the first thing to register as I lift from the darkness. *Cole.*

"I..." Luxxe is at a loss for words.

"You guys saw that, right? She just... disappeared." *Taylor.*

"That's crazy, though," Cole says, though I know by the sound of his voice he agrees with her.

I try to speak, to ask who they're talking about, but I'm still paralyzed. At least the strange burning inside is gone. What happened to me?

The next thing to register is a dull throb in my right leg. My knee. A pulse of pain shoots up my thigh and spreads into my limbs. I remember where I am now – the forest. And I'm lying on the ground. A stone digs into my right shoulder, and my body aches mercilessly. I moan a little. I've definitely felt better.

"Mira?" Luxxe says, gently tapping my cheek, "Mira, you okay?"

My eyes flutter open to see them staring down at me with a mixture of awe, concern, and total shock. "What?" I ask weakly.

"You *okay?*"

"Mostly. What happened?"

"You..." Words fail him again. I can't tell if he's freaked out or worried.

"You disappeared," Cole supplies.

"And we found you lying over here," Taylor adds.

I consider what they're saying for a moment, and then try to translate. Make sense of it. "Disappear? Like camouflage?"

Luxxe shakes his head.

Cole rubs the tension from his neck. "Disappear as in literally... into thin air."

They aren't making any sense. I'd think they were trying to prank me if Luxxe didn't look like he was nearing a panic attack.

I prop up on my elbow and my head spins. Cole catches me before I fall back again. "Whoa..." he soothes.

"I'm fine," I insist and push to stand. I wobble. Good thing Cole still has my arm. When my feet are steady, I wince from the pain still pounding into my right knee.

"What?" Luxxe says, appraising me for any signs of harm.

"I'm okay," I lie. "Just sprained my knee."

He squats to look at the leg I'm favoring. Not that he can see much through my jeans.

"Maybe when she landed over here she fell on it wrong," Taylor says.

Luxxe lightly feels around my kneecap. "No swelling yet."

"Let's go," I say. "I want to get back to Jacks."

Luxxe shoots me a smile, though it doesn't touch his eyes. He's scared for me. Whatever he thinks happened has frightened him. "All right. Let's get you back."

"You okay to walk?" Cole asks. "I can carry you."

"Yeah, I'm good," I say and pull away from him. I'd rather limp all the way back than have everyone see him carrying me into camp like some damsel in distress.

Cole hovers beside me as I find my footing but doesn't argue. "You're a tough one," he says as he watches me. "You know that?"

"She may not be a fighter," Luxxe adds, straightening and heading to collect the dead boar, "But she grew up with two boys. Of course, she's tough."

It's near dark when we make it back. Between Cole and Luxxe taking turns dragging the boar and my limping, it took twice as long. It was also unusually silent. Typically, Cole and Luxxe banter and reminisce about the hunt, but there was nothing to celebrate this time. I can't help the succinct feeling that I ruined what was supposed to be a fun evening, and I'd almost feel guilty if I wasn't so worried about what the hell happened to me.

I can't get the burning out of my mind. I remember the panic, which is normal when a boar's coming at me like a steam engine. But the pain... the heat tearing at my insides as it roiled inside me, and then darkness. Was that when I...?

It still seems ridiculous to even think it. *Disappeared.* And then apparently reappeared farther away.

I try to remember anything else that might help me make sense of it all, but everything is lost in the turmoil of the moment. I only remember how I felt and the eyes and tusks of the boar.

It's over, I remind myself. I need to let it go for now. I just want to get cleaned up and go to bed.

I prop against a tree at the edge of the clearing to rest before my trek home, watching as Luxxe and Taylor tug the boar to where the other carcasses are hanging. Ironically, I still mourn the boar's death, even after he tried to kill me. He had a family he was trying to protect. At least his meat and hide will be put to good use. Tonight, everyone will gut and skin them. Tomorrow, we'll feast.

I don't stick around for the gut-fest.

"You headed home?" Cole asks. The golden hue of the bonfire dances over his muscles, throwing shadows that seem to make each one impossibly bigger. Godlike. Even the sharp angles of his face and his squared jaw scream divinity.

Changers have some good genes. Genes that had apparently skipped right over me.

"Yeah," I say, moving my attention to the Elders beside the fire. I don't want him or anyone else to think I'm gawking. The Elders sit on logs, a crowd gathering around them. When everyone makes it back from the hunt, they'll tell stories about their old planet. Blythe and Jonah were only fifteen or so when our kind escaped to come here, but with the help of some of the older Changers, they tell us what they can remember.

Luxxe has told me a few things. Their planet was a lot like ours... well, like ours before the Great Disaster... with even more land. They had woodland tribes, which is the tribe Blythe and Jonah and my father was from, desert tribes, and tribes that lived in the mountains. Their woodland animals were also similar to ours, but different — coyotes as large as grizzlies and ten times as mean; deer-like creatures but with shorter snouts and showier antlers; snakes with two heads and jewel-tone scales. They were a delicacy and their skins used for clothes. I know there's more, but I can't possibly remember them all.

Though I never have because of the blood and guts, sticking around after the hunt sometimes appeals to me — I hear Jonah has a way of engrossing you in a story — but definitely not tonight. The only story I'm interested in involves me and my bed.

"You need help?" Cole asks.

I assess my injured knee, now slightly tight beneath my jeans (which probably means swollen), and because I've been relying on my right leg to do most of the work, it's shaking with exhaustion. Can I really hobble for another half hour without help? I suppose so, but I'm already nearing my threshold.

"Let me carry you or something," Cole suggests. "You have to be tired."

I am, but I can't find the words to actually *ask* for help. Besides, I still don't want anyone seeing him carry me. Torn, I just look at him.

He chuckles, knowing I won't ask. "Here," he says, sweeping me into a cradle of muscles and warmth before I have a chance to protest, "Let's get you back."

I contemplate an argument or suggesting he help steady me as I try and walk instead, but it's *so* good to be off my feet. I relax in his arms.

Who cares what people think?

Chapter 11

Illuminating our way, moonlight washes over the worn dirt path heading home, and I have to admit, despite the hurt knee and feeling a little humiliated being carried like a child, the journey back has been much more pleasant. Like Luxxe was before, Cole has been mostly silent, but his is more of a relaxed silence, even in his pondering. I would bet an entire season's worth of vegetables he's wondering about my mysterious disappearing act. But I don't ask; I'd rather not talk about it.

As we round the last bend, I already see the candlelight inside our cabin flagging us down. Maggie likes to weave baskets by it once darkness falls. *Almost there.* "Thank you for carrying me," I say. If I'd attempted this on my own, I'd have regretted it.

"Oh, God!" he says, pretending to be startled. He gives me droll smile. "Forgot I was carrying you for a moment; you weigh nothing. And you're welcome."

I nudge into him. "Real funny." But I'm sure there's a lot of truth to that. Compared to him, I'm feather light. "And sorry if you're angry with me about the boar," I add. I don't regret trying to save the boar initially, but I don't want him to be mad at me either. He lost an arrow because of me. I've never seen Cole's cheeks burn that red before. He's usually the yin to Luxxe's yang; polar opposites in temperament.

It takes him a minute to remember what I'm referring to, and realization crosses his face. "It's okay. I wasn't mad."

I raise my eyebrows at him with a smirk, waiting for the truth. He's so full of it.

His chest bounces against me as he laughs. "Okay, maybe I was a little mad, but not at you."

I hold my expression.

"Okay, maybe I was when you caused me to miss and I lost an arrow. It's all right, though. I'll make another one."

"Well, for what it's worth, I'm sorry."

"It's fine."

My thoughts spiral back to my... disappearance and silence lengthens between us. I know he's thinking about it again too.

"Sure you're okay?" he asks. All humor in his voice is gone.

"I'll live," I say casually, avoiding what I'm sure he really means. "I'll ask Maggie to help me wrap it later."

He pauses for a beat. "I meant the other thing."

Great. *Am* I okay? "Yeah," I answer. Weirded out? Most definitely. But I'm okay.

"What was it like?"

I try to remember, but all I can recall is blurs of burning and darkness, then waking up. I shrug, still not up for talking about it. "Don't really know."

He eyes me warily. "Don't know as in don't remember?"

I shake my head.

Spectacle

He's quiet again, and I think he gets the hint until he says, "Honestly, it was…" He searches for the right words. "…pretty damn cool."

I tilt my head at him. "Cool?"

"Yeah," he says thoughtfully. "Like some kind of superhero move. Like you teleported."

I huff a small laugh. What a guy thing to say. "Well, I don't feel like a superhero." I feel like a freak, to be honest. As if I'm not already different enough from the others.

"Think you could do it again?"

"Not if I can help it."

We arrive, and he lowers me down, gripping my arm until I'm steady. "Fair enough," he says. "Will we see you tomorrow?" he asks expectantly. There's more to his question than just casual pleasantry, but I can't put my finger on it. Maybe my *superhero* move has him hoping to see more. Maybe next time I'll shoot lasers from my eyes.

"Yeah, I'll be there," I say.

"Good," he says and pulls me into a long side-hug. "See you then, Mira."

"See you then," I reply and watch as he lumbers away. "And, Cole?"

"Yep?" he says, turning to walk backward.

"Please don't say anything to anyone. And tell Luxxe and Taylor not to either."

"Got it covered," he says, winking, and turns to sprint down the path.

Watching as the velvety black beneath the canopy of trees swallows him whole, I decide to savor a few minutes alone in the dark before I have to limp inside. I sigh, lifting my face to the starlit heavens to find some solace there. What a hell of a day.

And yet with neither love nor hate,
Those stars like some snow-white
Minerva's snow-white marble eyes
Without the gift of sight.

Maggie's soft voice rolls in behind me and jars me from the moment. "Need help?"

I hobble to face her, and she's already on her way. "Twisted knee," I say, embarrassed.

"That would explain Cole carrying you, then." She slips her arm under me for support, and I wonder if she overheard our conversation. We weren't far when Cole started with the superhero talk. If she did, she isn't letting on. "I'm guessing Luxxe is gutting whatever he killed?"

I grimace. *Ugh.* "Yeah, probably."

"Let's get you cleaned up. Then we'll tend to that knee."

"I'm surprised you didn't try and make it home without help," Maggie says from the other room. I can tell by her calm, measured voice she's concentrating on weaving. Leg elevated, I soak in our washtub to get the grit and boy-sweat off me. Though I tell her it's not necessary, she always has a hot bath waiting for me when I return. I know how many trips to the creek and pots of water she has to boil to make it happen. But she always does. It's the mother in her.

"Cole insisted," I say and wash a handful of water up my side. The lavender-scented suds leave my skin clean and fragrant.

"Nice of him."

"Yeah."

I dunk a cloth in the water and scrub my face and shoulders. Feels amazing after a long, sweaty, tiresome day, the steam and lavender relaxing my tense and knotted places. I sigh and retreat further into the tub.

In the room across from Maggie, Jacks is snoring lightly, and his feet twitch with sleep in the candlelight. Maybe he's dreaming of a better place. Maybe he's dreaming of our younger days when he could get around easier and had the love of his parents to soothe his fears and worries.

I hope we're enough for him now. I hope his mom would be proud.

Spectacle

"Do you like him?" Maggie asks.

Her question derails my thoughts. "Um... what?"

"*Like* him," she repeats.

"Cole?"

She chuckles. "Yes, dear."

"I... I guess he's all right."

"Just all right?" The way she asks makes me think she expected more enthusiasm, and it dawns on me how she meant it — if I like him as more than a friend. "Yeah, he's a friend," I finally reply.

"Then I'll quit prying," she concedes. "I know you're a private person. Just looked like he might think of *you* as more than a friend, is all."

Embarrassed, my cheeks flush with heat. "Really?" I think back to our parting conversation, and I don't remember anything out of the ordinary. He's always been polite and helpful. But was Maggie right? Did Cole think of me as more?

"I do," she says, and I let her words hang in the air. I don't have the patience to worry about it tonight.

After washing, Maggie helps me into an oversized t-shirt and onto my mat. She cuts a stained shirt I usually reserve for gardening into strips and kneels, wrapping it around my knee. Her nimble hands, well-suited for her trade, have the bandage snug around my leg in no time. "I'll save the scraps," she says and tosses them into my clothes bin — one of her creations. "You can use them to clean dishes."

Wasting anything around here is a sin.

As she gathers the baskets she weaved, I make good use of the remaining candlelight by reading the only book I have to my name — the book of Frost poems I brought with me the day we were exiled. I cling to them like life rafts. They're the only ones I can recite anymore. Keats' and Woolf's and Poe's words are lost to the haze of time. Every now and then, I'll remember a line or two, and if I'm lucky, an entire passage. Even then I'm sure I get some of the words wrong.

"Goodnight, Mira," Maggie says sweetly, brushing the hair from my forehead and then straightening. She turns for the door, her baskets tucked under her arm. "I'll see you before sunrise."

I yawn my reply. "You will?"

"Tomorrow's Commencement Day," she says matter-of-factly, and she's gone. She leaves me with a nauseating stir in my stomach, staring at the empty doorframe and clutching my book so hard my nails are digging into the leather. Commencement Day already? Has it been six months?

Tomorrow the men in uniform will be here, and tomorrow, more Changers will volunteer to be whisked away on a helicopter never to be seen again.

Chapter 12

I awake during the night with a start. My dreams were fractured and heavy with disturbing images. They started with the piglets in the woods, running and frantic, and unable to find their father. I found myself crying for them in their loneliness and utter despair. Then I see their dad, alive and back in the woods with me and our hunting crew. The boar looks at me and there's innocence in his eyes. He's observing. But bloodlust has overtaken Luxxe again, his lips pulled back from his teeth in a snarl. He wants to claim him and rob his family of his life.

He wants the boar dead.

I cry out to save him, but Luxxe doesn't care. He wants him for his own selfish reasons. He raises the spear, and the hog backs into a tree, scared but with nowhere to go as Cole and Taylor crowd around him. I feel his despair. His silent pleas to spare his life.

In my desperation to save the hog, I see flashes of my father's face again. An innocent killed too soon. An innocent's family robbed of their patriarch.

In a blaze of muscle and sweat, the spear lunges into its neck, and all goes black. My cries echo into the void.

As if someone hits rewind, we're back again. The hog is alive, but he's angry this time. Rage rolls from his body like an intoxicating mist, and I can't help but be angry as well. Some injustice has been done. Someone I love is being wronged. Someone needs to pay.

I look in synchronization with the hog at Luxxe, the same greedy snarl on Luxxe's face. But for all the hog's hatred, he's still powerless, and though he tries to charge, Luxxe kills him all the same.

His fate was always death, and his kids were meant to be alone.

A tear travels along my cheek, and I angrily swipe it away. Despite the boar's intent - innocence or animosity - is it still considered 'fate' if its death is at the hands of someone wicked and full of greed? At that point, is it not cold-hearted murder? Fate wouldn't want that. Murder is taking things into your own hands. Claiming what isn't yours.

I release a heavy sigh, rolling to my side. I don't know why I ponder these things, but they're there. Though I never admit it to anyone, including myself, I'd like to know, one day, why my father's life was taken. The only thing I can fathom is some unjust reason.

But I'm sure I'll never know.

What difference would it make anyway? Like the piglets, my life will always seem a little aimless, a little lonelier because of the void in it.

I clasp my pendant tighter and try not to think of my parents or animals, or anything warm and lovely from my past. It's not there anymore. It's not. All of it is gone. I know this because, at night, when I find myself teetering between consciousness and sleep, when wisps of my father's memory kiss my nose before bed, the loneliness finds me there. And when tears are budding in my eyes, I push them away and let the numbness take me again to rescue me from the sorrow.

Then, tomorrow, I'll wake and busy myself with my purposes here and convince myself everything is okay. After everything, we're okay.

Footsteps outside wake me, and I know whose they must be – Maggie's. The darkness is too saturated for it to be morning, though. She came early. Maybe she couldn't sleep. I roll to my stomach with a groan and bury my face in the bend of my arm. Just a few more minutes....

As I slip back under, the apparitions of my last dream flicker behind my eyelids - Jacks and I in our old life. It's winter and he's healthier, the cold nipping our noses until they're glowing pink. We're making a snowman and laughing uncontrollably as he sticks a carrot on it in an inappropriate place.

I smile.

Lifting me into consciousness again, the ground beneath me vibrates. She's inside. I expect a candle to flicker to life, so she can see what she's doing. On Commencement Day, she usually fixes breakfast and waits with us for Luxxe and his friends to arrive. They'll be bringing a stretcher Maggie designed to transport Jacks; it has a strong wooden frame and a woven bamboo center. The only time we use it is for feasts, when he feels up to them, and Commencement Day.

But the flame doesn't come. "Hello?" I say into the darkness, my voice thick with sleep.

A voice beside me answers. "Hey."

I yelp, scooting back on my mat. It isn't Maggie.

"It's me," Nolie whispers.

I blink up at her, adjusting my eyes to the darkness, and her form slowly takes shape. Her hacked-up hair sticks out on the side from where she slept, her puffy eyes squinting to try and read my reaction. I release the breath I'm holding. "What's wrong?" I ask. "Does your mom know you're here?"

She shakes her head gently.

"Bad dreams again?" I ask. Before Jacks' mom died, Nolie used to curl up beside her when she had nightmares. She was like a second mother to her. To all of us. Nolie's mom sleeps so soundly. Thanks to her perpetual drunken stupor, she can't even wake her for comfort.

Nolie nods, and a sliver of moonlight peeking through my curtain glints off her tears. She looks younger when she's wrapped in vulnerability. "Want to lie down with me?" I offer. I don't sleep well with someone beside me, but my heart aches for her.

Nodding again, she holds up something limp and furry. "I brought you a squirrel."

I pause. "Thanks?" I finally manage. I hope my look of humored disgust doesn't show through the dark. How long has that thing been dead?

She lowers to my mat, scooting to lay flush against my belly like my dog, Trevor, used to. I push those memories away. "Night, Bella," she yawns.

"Night, Noles..." *You sweet, weird kid.*

Someone pokes my cheek, and I groan, unready to wake.

Hushed laughter fills the air. I groan again.

Another poke, then a wet finger prods my ear. I gasp and sling my elbow. It strikes something solid with a crack. "Ow!" Luxxe howls, and another boy's voice — at least I assume it belongs to a boy — squeals with terror in the background.

Bleary-eyed and pissed, I catapult to a sitting position, and it takes me a good minute to get my bearings. Luxxe is cupping his nose with both hands, blood dribbling in streamers down his neck and chest. He's glaring at me through glassy eyes. "Geez, Mira! What the hell."

"*Luxxe,*" Maggie scolds.

Spectacle

My attention snaps to Cole, doubled over and laughing his barky laugh. On the floor across from me, Jacks is laughing so hard nothing comes out. I then pinpoint the owner of the squeaky girl-scream – Riddick. He's beet red, but not with anger like Luxxe, more like crippling embarrassment.

My eyes sweep back over them as I wipe the slobber from my ear. I narrow them on Luxxe, the wet-willy offender.

"You broke my nose," he says, his hands muffling the words.

Maggie offers him a cloth. "You're fine," she says. "That's what you get for messing with her."

I stifle a laugh. She's right. But as Luxxe waits expectantly for me to say something, I stare at him, unsure if I'm remorseful or justified. Hell... I'm barely awake yet. And a little pissed.

Furious, he snatches the cloth and storms out to nurse his pride and his nose. I eye Maggie. I can tell she wants to follow after him and give him something real to pout over, but she lets him go and mumbles under her breath about teenage boys and their hormones. Her attention turns to me. "He'll be fine, dear," she says.

"I didn't mean to," I say.

"I know."

Cole's coughing draws our attention back to him. He's laughing so hard he's nearly choking. He points at Riddick. "Dude!" he says between gasps. "You're afraid of *squirrels*."

Squirrels? I look to Maggie questioningly and she shrugs.

"Shut up, man," Riddick grumbles. He crosses his arms tight over his chest, and if it's possible, his cheeks are redder.

On the floor behind them, Jacks picks up the offending, bushy carcass by the leg and dangles it in Riddick's direction. "Better run! It's gonna get yooou..." he teases. Cole laughs harder.

My memories spiral back to the middle of the night. Nolie brought it to me. Why, I don't know.

"Where did it come from?" Maggie asks.

Riddick nods in my direction. "Mira was sleeping with it," He says it accusatorily.

"I was *not*," I replied. "Nolie brought it to me last night."

Cole drags in a breath, holding his stomach to try and get himself together. "You kinda were," he says. "And then when you-" He bursts into laughter again.

"And then when you swung your arm at Luxxe," Jacks supplies for him. "The squirrel went flying at Riddick."

"And then he screamed like a little girl!" Cole finishes.

Riddick waits for my reaction, and I bite my lips together to keep a straight face. Big, tough Riddick – a hunter like the others. And Luxxe's twin, if it weren't for the reddish hue in his dreads and cleft chin. And apparently, he's scared of squirrels.

He'll *never* live this down.

Chapter 13

Our bi-annual trek to the pasture for the Commencement Day ceremony is one I should enjoy. Especially on a day like today, when the clouds shroud the sun in a thick blanket, the blossoming midday heat somewhat bearable. On any other day, going to any other place, I'd be smiling. But I can never bring myself to. One would think the vibrant smile on Jacks' face, as the boys carry him on the stretcher, would be enough to evoke a similar one on mine. He loves getting out of the cabin and feeling the breeze and sunlight caress his skin; he gets so little of either these days. Even the boys' banter — this time about Riddick's squirrel phobia — should induce some sort of delighted response from me. But not these days.

I'd suffer through a hundred yesterdays, twisted knee and all, to avoid them. The only reason I don't? Because of the boy on the stretcher. He lives for Commencement Day, and they only come twice a year. So, I suck it up. I'm even using crutches Maggie brought me, so I can be here with him.

"I think the lanky kid from the mountain tribe will volunteer again," Jacks says. "He looked so disappointed when they chose Emerson last time."

I smile a little. *Here we go.* Part of the thrill for Jacks is speculating who will volunteer and who will actually be chosen.

"My money's on the crazy-looking chick from the desert tribe," replies Cole. "But I know who *wouldn't* have a chance at being picked…"

Jacks snorts, trying to hold back his laughter.

"Sissies who're afraid of animals."

Riddick scoffs. "That stopped being funny about twenty jokes ago, man."

"I agree," Luxxe mumbles.

We all look to him in synchronization. He hasn't said much, and I have a feeling it has nothing to do with his nose. He went back to whatever dark and gloomy place he was at yesterday when he wanted to tell me something but couldn't. If he doesn't tell me by the end of today, I'll pester him until he does. Or threaten him with my very capable elbow.

"Oh, so you *can* speak," Jacks notes. "Thought you'd lost your voice."

Luxxe ignores him, and everyone falls into silence.

With nothing to listen to now but the thrum of our footsteps and the occasional buzz of an insect, my thoughts swirl around who might volunteer from *our* tribe… not that it'll matter. This is the sixth Commencement Day and no volunteers from our tribe have been chosen so far. Maybe they think of us as little woodland elves that prance around eating leaves. I guess *desert* and *mountain* tribes do have meaner rings to them. Not that the tribal names have anything to do with where we live anymore. We're all on one island, just separated into the tribes of our ancestors. Nobody dictated that was the way it needed to be. Each tribe has different traditions and ways of living than the other, so it was more of a natural progression.

Spectacle

There is one thing we all have in common, though – a chance to enter into a Freedom Match.

Three years ago, men in uniform stormed into our villages with rifles and forced us to listen to a proposition. A proposition some of our kind couldn't resist. A proposition I consider sick and insulting.

A newly formed corporation, FM Incorporated, dreamed up an event called a Freedom Match, and the idea is that if one of our kind wants to leave the island and live among the citizens of New America again, they'd have to fight, gladiator-style, to the death with another opponent – a human opponent the corporation hand picks and trains. And apparently, according to the soldiers and corporate representative who paid us a visit, FM Incorporated was given the government's approval to do so.

Freedom Matches are held every six months, and two weeks before each one, on Commencement Day, soldiers fly in on helicopters with FM employees who take pictures and get the biographies of the Changers who are salivating at the opportunity to go back to New America. They're usually the ones who want to be reunited with those they were forced to leave behind –friends, soul mates, human family members. Someone like me, if my mother hadn't...

Once the representatives get the information on all the candidates, the New American citizens vote for their favorite contender, and two weeks later, a helicopter comes back to cart the chosen one away. But we never know the outcome because televisions and radios are non-existent here, which is fine by me. I'd rather not know. It sickens me to think one of us is exploited to the public, someone who's lovesick for home and whoever awaits them there, so this company can make their millions. Whether they volunteer for it or not.

We're told Freedom Matches are held in an old football stadium and are considered one of the biggest events and revenue makers of New America's existence. Luxxe's mom suspects the government gets a cut of it. More than just the taxes they would pay on revenue. Otherwise, why would they okay something like this when we're so *dangerous?* Maybe, according to the FM representatives, because we're promised an apartment in a building reserved for the winners and their human loves ones, and all their needs are taken care of by FM Incorporated. There's no need to mingle with the public, and when there is, they're escorted by an FM bodyguard.

It would almost sound tempting if I wasn't so revolted by it. And by no means a warrior. But I do often ask myself, if I knew my mother was still alive, what would *I* do for the chance to see her again? Probably go through hell and back. Probably what these poor souls do: volunteer for a chance to fight for their freedom every six months.

As we cross through the creek bed, I expect to hear the familiar rumbling of a crowd in the distance, like the oscillating, fervent hum of a beehive. All Changers aren't expected to show, but most do. Like Jacks, they have a morbid curiosity for who will volunteer. But today, I don't hear anything.

Jacks and I look at each other.

"It is today, right?" Riddick asks, echoing my thoughts.

"Yeah," Maggie answers. "It's been exactly six months."

"And we all heard the helicopters a few mornings ago," Cole adds.

I purse my lips. *They* must have heard them, but maybe I was still asleep. Which is part of the reason Commencement Day snuck up on me this time.

I see glimpses of the white FM Incorporated tents through the trees as we near the pasture ahead, which means everything has been set up as usual. So, the silence is definitely weird. Borderline unsettling. Over half of the Changers should already be there. And judging by the stray rays of sunlight finding their way through cracks in the clouds, the sun isn't even at its highest, which means we're a little early, but not *that* early.

We trudge on anyway, the boys winded now from carrying Jacks so long. They're like pack mules, though – sturdy and resilient. They have hours before crying mercy and we're only minutes away.

The closer we get, the more I hear *something*, though it's not the typical crowd noise. More like the murmur of a stream – urgent but hushed. Whispers?

Spectacle

When we break through the tree line into the clearing, the pasture full of Changers eases our worry. Only slightly. We now understand the shift in the atmosphere and cause of the fevered whispers: a stage, three times longer than the other, demands its place along the far end of the field. Black boxes on poles are positioned on either side of it, and two microphone stands sit lonely in the center. Serving as the backdrop, three white banners hang behind it, each one representing a tribe with their respective symbols - one for the woodland tribe, a bare tree with twisted branches reaching for the heavens; one for the desert tribe, a rattlesnake skeleton poised to strike. Lastly, a buck reared on its hind legs and impressive antlers for the mountain tribe. Seeing them displayed by FM on their glossy fabric with fancy black ink makes my teeth grind in anger. These symbols are sacred, a piece of our heritage from a planet far away. Our tribe etches the tree into wooden jewelry as a reminder of where we came from, who we are; it's not for *them* to use at their disposal. To celebrate what they're doing.

"They're filming it this time!" Jacks enthuses.

My gaze travels to the front of the stage to see a metal fence surrounding men with expensive-looking camera equipment. They're filming the ceremony. But why?

"Means they're making good money off of us," Maggie grumbles, then adds with sarcasm, "Time to ramp up production."

More disgusted than ever, all I can do is shake my head, and I look to Luxxe for his reaction. His eyes, flared wide, are fixed on the indulgent set-up ahead, his face blanched. The muscles along his jawline are flickering as he clenches his teeth. He's spooked but straining to keep his composure.

He never gets spooked.

His reaction has my stomach flipping over itself. After being friends with him for so long, I've learned this – if Luxxe is concerned about something, there's cause to be concerned. He might be hot-headed. He might be impatient. But above everything, he's brave.

Something's going on.

Despite my churning insides, I remain stoic. He's obviously trying to hide his reaction from us and I don't want to let on I'm picking up on his little *moment*. But I can't help wondering why. If something's off, why wouldn't he tell us? I can only trust he would if he felt the need to. I've also learned this about my friend – I can trust him completely.

When we meet the back of the crowd, Riddick, holding one side at the front of the stretcher, slows. "This looks like a good spot," he says. Luxxe and Cole grunt their agreement and they lower Jacks to the ground. By the time the rest arrive and settle in behind us, we'll be dead center.

Until then, I plant myself beside Jacks, my crutches in the grass beside me, and wait for the absurdly enthusiastic man and his near-fluorescent smile to announce when the ceremony has begun. I'd rather not look at the display ahead of us any longer than I have to. The display our brethren paid for with their bloody, gruesome deaths, or someone else's.

Here's to "freedom."

Chapter 14

The speakers buzz to life with static – a harsh, unnatural sound in the wilderness – and a hush falls over the crowd. It must be time. Cole and Luxxe help Jacks onto Riddick's shoulders so he can see.

I stand with the aid of my crutches, slow and begrudging, contemplating staying seated, but I can either hide at the underbelly of the crowd or face what I know is happening anyway. At least I'm shorter than most everyone around me and only see glimpses when people shift on their feet.

The person in front of me bends to scratch their ankle, and I see FM's enthusiastic front man and Commencement Day host - Ricardo. He's kneeling at the edge of the stage and speaking to a woman with a clipboard and a headset. I have to cover my mouth to keep from laughing. I can't decide which is tackier this time – Ricardo's glowing teeth or his black sequined suit. His mohawk, taller than before with streaks of blue, towers in a perfect crest above his feminine face. I swear he's wearing eyeliner.

The person in front of me straightens again, and Ricardo's gone. But I keep my eyes forward, knowing if they wander to the sides of the stage I'll see the men in uniform who come to keep the FM employees "safe." Just the possibility of seeing them, just knowing they're there, stirs anger inside me. Every foul memory I have surrounding both of my parents' deaths involves men in uniform. While I know these men aren't personally responsible, I can't help the rage exploding inside me when I lay eyes on them. Like the sorrow, I try to keep it tucked away. Anger leads to violence, and that's why we're here. Anger and violence and fearing the unfamiliar; it only breeds pain and destruction.

A microphone squeals, and I jump. "New Americaaaa!" Ricardo belts out. His Spanish accent seems thicker this time. "Welcome to Changer Island."

Curious, I raise up on the balls of my feet. He hasn't opened a ceremony that way before. He's looking straight into one of the cameras, one hand clutching a microphone, the other reaching for the sky. His open smile is splitting his face in two.

I lower, rolling my eyes. So, they've named the place we were exiled to. *Changer Island*. How sweet. My gaze shifts to Luxxe, hand in hand with Taylor. I can tell he's still fighting whatever's upsetting him.

"Hey," Cole whispers in my ear. "Want up on my shoulders?" His eyes have that excited sparkle to them again, similar to the one before a hunt. I'll never understand these boys' delight in watching people volunteer for something so awful. I shake my head and move my gaze forward again. "Suit yourself," he says, giving my shoulder a friendly squeeze. His hand lingers there longer than necessary.

Behind us, Maggie chuckles, and I feel her eyes on us. I hate knowing what she thinks of me and Cole now – possible lovebirds. I shift awkwardly on my crutches.

The beginning of the ceremony runs slower than normal. Normally, Ricardo thanks us for coming and calls volunteers to the

Spectacle

stage for pictures and questions about their talents and history, anything that might make them a suitable opponent. But today, he wants to run through multiple takes of the scripted intro to make sure they get the best possible one. I wonder if everyone else around me has the same urge to yell out insults or profanities each time the cameras roll so there's nothing they can use. The thought brings a droll smile to my face, and I'd almost consider it if I didn't think one of the men in uniform would eventually intervene. I don't want them anywhere near me.

Finally, we get to the part where Ricardo asks for volunteers, and hands pop up. I count more than five from where I'm standing. Ricardo points to someone near the front, and I move to peer between two people in front of me and see the crazy-looking girl from the desert tribe making her way to the stage. Ricardo pulls her up, then immediately wipes his hands on a handkerchief in his back pocket.

I huff a laugh through my nose. *What's wrong, pretty boy? Don't want to get Changer cooties?*

"Joanna!" Ricardo enthuses. "Good to see you again, mi querida."

Joanna regards him with an eat-shit-and-die look, and the crowd snickers quietly. Ricardo continues without missing a beat. "And I see you've made some..." He searches for the right words, and by the looks of his tentative expression, words that won't provoke her to snap his skinny little neck in two. "...*improvements* to your look."

Proud he mentioned it, she flashes a devilish smile and straightens her bone necklace – customary jewelry for the desert tribe. This time, she made a point to wear one with a rabbit skull in the center, and smaller skulls, probably squirrels, and mice, circle up around her neck. Her hair, which she usually wears like the rest of them in short knobby dreads, is grown out and unkempt like she hadn't bothered to maintain it. It definitely gives her a more... *wild* appearance. But what tops off her look is the black war paint she smudged around her eyes and down her cheeks.

Cole murmurs under his breath. "She's *so* getting picked this year."

"She's definitely trying hard to get picked," I reply.

"Tell me, Joanna," Ricardo continues, eying her necklace, "I see you're still a skilled hunter. Remind us, what weapons are you an expert with?"

She smiles wider and looks straight into the camera. "I can kill anything with anything."

Ricardo laughs boisterously. "I'm sure you can, dear. I'm sure you can. And remind us of your age again?"

"Eighteen."

"Wonderful," he says, and gestures for someone's assistance.

A girl appears on stage, her black evening dress sequined like Ricardo's suit. Her winged eyeliner streaks out to her temples, and when she blinks, her eyelids reveal flashes of silver to match the dozens of rings and studs in her ears.

The girl takes Joanna by the elbow.

"Thank you, Joanna," Ricardo says, and the girl ushers her to the back of the stage. "Who's next?" he asks, craning his neck to scan the crowd.

One by one, the other volunteers join him on stage. There aren't as many this time, but still plenty for New America to choose from. Most of them are around our age, but some are older, some so young they wouldn't possibly be considered. Even Jacks' favorite - the lanky kid from the mountain tribe - volunteers. Like Joanna, he played up his looks in an effort to get selected. He shaved his hair into a wide, flat mohawk and a coyote pelt drapes around his shoulders. Not sure it's enough to beat Joanna, though.

"Is that all, then?" Ricardo asks, his eyes filled with disappointment. Guess he was hoping for more camera time. "Anyone else?"

We look around at one another. No one else wants to be whisked away to kill or be killed? Anyone? *Surprising.*

I turn to see if the people behind us have started dispersing yet. I'd love to have some time at home before the feast tonight.

"Me," someone says, and the voice sends a jolt up my spine. Slowly, I turn back around, and my eyes lock to the back of his head. "Me," Luxxe repeats. "I volunteer."

Spectacle

Chapter 15

I must have gone into shock between the time Luxxe volunteered and climbed the stage, because I don't remember him making his way there. When I snap back to reality, it hurls into me like a taut rubber band, and I gasp. I immediately look to Maggie, her face pallid white, then to Taylor, but her back is to me. Hoping this is a sick joke they're all in on, I search the boys' faces as well. They, too, look like they're in some freaky alternate reality.

Is this really happening?

My supporting leg starts to shake, even with the crutches, and I clutch onto the first sturdy thing within reach – Cole's arm. He doesn't seem to notice, his eyes trained on Luxxe and Ricardo. "Cole," I say, tugging his arm, "I want on your shoulders."

He doesn't acknowledge me... or can't hear me through his own shock.

Spectacle

"*Cole.*"

He jerks out of it, bending without a word, and helps me onto his shoulders. When he straightens, Luxxe's eyes meet mine. Whatever expression I'm wearing causes him to wince, but he quickly recovers.

"Tell us your name," Ricardo begins. He dabs the handkerchief across his brow, the midday humidity getting to him inside his dark suit.

Luxxe's eyes nervously flicker to the camera. "Solomon," he replies.

Solomon?

Why would he use his first name? He *hates* that name. Just as puzzled, Jacks looks at me from Riddick's shoulders.

"Solomon..." Ricardo repeats. He gives Luxxe the once-over; a child standing next to a giant. A smile spreads across Ricardo's face. "Maybe we'll call you Goliath instead."

Laughter rolls from the crowd, from those of us able to react at all, and Luxxe tries to force a smile.

"So, Goliath," Ricardo continues. More laughter. "How old are you?"

He clears his throat. "Sixteen."

Ricardo gapes. "*Sixteen?*"

He nods.

"My..." he says, appraising him again, "...our youngest volunteer today. And the biggest."

Maggie whimpers behind us. "Someone stop this," she says, her voice strained. Cole holds my legs with one arm and reaches to pull her into him with the other. We all know once Luxxe is on stage, to interfere would mean facing the men in uniform.

"Are you a hunter? Are you good with any weapons?" Ricardo squeezes Luxxe's bicep, giving a silent "wow" to the crowd. "By the looks of it, you could probably just sit on your prey."

Luxxe gives a curt nod and pulls his shoulders back, seemingly finding his confidence. "I actually teach our tribe to hunt."

Ricardo raises his eyebrows to the camera. "Did you hear that, New America? Goliath is only sixteen and is already training others how to hunt." He dabs his forehead again. "Now, let's..." His words trail, and he squints at Luxxe's nose, leaning closer.

Luxxe pulls back.

"Is that..." He cocks his head. "Did someone break your nose?"

Luxxe's jaw twitches, but he keeps a straight face. "My nose?"

"Uh, *yeah*..." he says, circling his finger at it dramatically, "Either that or you borrowed a little of Joanna's war paint."

The crowd chuckles again, and that's when I notice it too – faint shadows underscoring his eyes and creeping onto the bridge of his nose. Not very obvious at first glance because of the blue markings. I'd feel guilty if I could feel anything but paralyzing shock.

"Oh, that..." Luxxe says dismissively. "It's nothing." He manages a half-smirk. "You should see the other guy."

Ricardo releases a belly laugh. "I'm sure!" He scans the crowd eagerly. "Where *is* the other guy? Does he have the guts to show himself?"

The cameras pan the crowd.

Luxxe shoots me a desperate *don't say anything* look.

"No?" Ricardo says. "Nobody wants to fess up to being pummeled by Goliath?"

"He probably didn't make it," Luxxe says. "I'd be surprised if he could walk."

I snort. *Right.*

"Well, there you have it, New America." Ricardo gives Luxxe an enthusiastic pat. "Looks like we have a true contender here!"

The others behind them roll their eyes, and Joanna looks like she wants to tear Ricardo's throat out. She probably would.

Triumphant, Luxxe looks at the cameras one last time, then the girl in the sequined dress escorts him to the back of the stage.

I focus on the sound of my feet pounding against the earth, ignoring the pain shooting through my leg with each footfall. I tossed my crutches minutes ago; they were slowing me down. After I wiggled

Spectacle

down from Cole's shoulders, I felt claustrophobic and panicky, so I had to get out of there. Now I'm racing home.

Keep breathing, I tell myself. When I think of what Luxxe has done, I forget. He's volunteering to abandon us.

It doesn't make sense.

Why? Why would you want to leave us, Luxxe? All your loved ones are here.

Breathe in. Breathe out.

The panic rises inside me, threatening to swallow me whole. He can't do this. He's needed here. *I* need him here!

I push myself faster, but my knee won't let me. I'm limping now.

Breathe in. Breathe out.

A tree root catches the foot of my injured leg, and I stumble. My face and shoulder hit the ground and I slide to a stop, the impact knocking the wind out of me. Spots dance in my vision and I try to suck in a lungful of air, but instead, I cough and sputter into the dirt.

Shakily, I push with my arms and manage to hold myself up on all fours. When I'm able to breathe again, I assess the damage. My shoulder feels okay, but my face – the budding sting above my right eyebrow tells me I scraped it.

I raise my head to look behind me. I need to keep going.

I attempt to stand, but my exhausted leg gives in. I try a second time and my leg won't even push me up. I cry out in frustration. Why did I throw away the damn crutches? Now I'm stuck here or I'm crawling home.

Stupid Luxxe. All of this is his fault. That traitor...

Desperation wells inside, consuming me, tears flooding my eyes. A sob bursts out of me against my will. I thought he loved us. I thought he was my friend. People don't leave the ones they love behind. They don't even *conceive* of it.

I don't understand.

What if he's chosen? What if he fights? He could...

"Mira!" a voice calls.

I shift on the ground to see who it is. *Cole.* As I watch him sprint toward me with the crutches slung over his shoulder, I can't decide if I'm annoyed or relieved. I was running away for a reason; I needed to be alone. But the closer he comes, I decide to let the annoyance go. I can't get home without the crutches.

He immediately falls to my side, his eyes roaming over me. I know I'm a mess — scraped up and dirty. "God, Mira, what happened?"

"Fell," I say, the word sounding more pitiful than intended. I take a broken breath. "Was trying to run home."

He looks at me with understanding, the shadows of hurt and betrayal playing across his features. He's mad at Luxxe too. "You all right?"

I shrug, a frown tugging at my lips. A leftover tear escapes.

"Well, let's get you home, then," he says sweetly and grasps my arm to help me stand.

"What about Jacks?" I say.

"It'll be fine. Luxxe and Riddick can handle it."

Chapter 16

"You didn't know either, huh?" I ask Cole. I try not to wince as I'm saying it; the crutches are biting into my armpits. He offered to carry me, but I refused. I can't spend the next week or so in someone's arms until my knee heals. I have to get used to lugging myself around.

"No," he sighs. "I didn't. Caught me off guard."

"Me too."

We continue on, brooding in silence, and a patch of flowers catches my eye. I don't know their name, but they're a wild shade of red and grow close to the path. We usually pick them for Tabitha's grave. I hobble over to them, but Cole beats me there. He gently collects enough for a bouquet. "Stop there first?" he asks, already knowing the answer.

I nod solemnly, feeling guilty I'd almost forgotten in the haze of my panic and sorrow. Visiting the graveyard is tradition on the way home from Commencement Day. We'll make our way there and wait for the others to catch up. I can stew in my emotions later tonight when Jacks is sleeping and I'm alone.

Storm clouds gather in the distance, and the wind is strong and untiring. I hold my braid, so the ends won't whip at my neck. At least we'll get a good rain tonight, which I'll welcome; I won't have to water my garden with a sore knee and the feast will be postponed. I can't fathom being around everyone after the news breaks of Luxxe volunteering. I imagine most will be as shocked and upset as us, and I have my own emotions to deal with.

"Why do you think he did it?" Cole asks. We sit on a flat rock by the entrance of the graveyard. His elbows rest on his knees, his head hanging as he absently kicks around a pebble.

"I wish I could tell you," I reply. "He hasn't said anything about it. But he has been acting weird."

He peers up at me with his squinty grey eyes. "You noticed it too?"

"Only yesterday and today. He seemed distracted on our way to the hunt. And when I called him out on it he denied anything was wrong."

"And he's been grumpier lately," he added.

"Definitely."

Cole returns to his pebble, and I watch the path for our friends. "You think this was a spur of the moment thing?" he asks.

"No," I reply, not needing to ponder over it. "Luxxe doesn't do that unless he's angry or hunting. He's been contemplating this."

Cole sighs, defeated. "I guess you're right. Just doesn't make sense."

I nod my agreement. No sense at all.

"At least nobody from a woodland tribe has ever been picked before," he adds. "Maybe he won't get chosen."

Spectacle

"True." Doesn't upset me any less, though.

Long minutes pass, and the wind grows stronger, the clouds darker. We finally hear footsteps. "About time," Cole grumbles, standing. He offers his hand to help me up and onto my crutches. First, we see Riddick, Jacks clinging to his back. Riddick holds his shriveled legs around his waist. Both of them look how I expect — confused and fresh with sorrow. Luxxe brings up the tail end, his eyes fixed on the ground. No Maggie. No Taylor. They must have headed back to camp with the stretcher.

As the boys approach, the initial shock of everything washes over me again. The shock then morphs to sorrow, then to anger. I don't consider pushing against it. Sometimes, unleashing it is justified. And Luxxe owes us some answers.

I start for him immediately, lips pursed. The heat in my cheeks is near searing. "Mira," Cole says, reaching after me, but thinks better of it.

When Riddick catches my expression, his eyes flare, and he steps aside. "Mira…" Jacks breathes, and I think he asks me what happened to my dirty, bloody face, but I'm too furious to process it. With every hobbling step toward Luxxe, I shake harder, the rage taking over.

Luxxe looks up at me and freezes. I drop my crutches, limp my last few steps, and shove him as hard as I can. "How dare you!" I try to yell, but it comes out as a strangled cry. I shove him again. "Tell me why!"

"Calm down," he says, reaching for my arms.

I swat him away.

"I can't right now… just-"

"Tell me! Tell me why you want to leave us."

He looks at me, his eyes heavy and remorseful. "I…"

Defiant tears break through, flowing warm and heavy, and I try to shove him again, but I have nothing left. "Tell me," I choke out, pleading.

His own eyes well. "I can't, Mira. Not right now." He reaches for me again, but I hobble out of reach. Frustrated, he rubs his neck with a sigh, his eyes pinching closed. A tear falls. "I really can't. I'm sorry."

"*Can't?* Says who?"

He presses his lips tight, that same infuriating look on his face as yesterday when he wanted to tell me but couldn't.

"Then when?" I sniffle.

"Maybe tonight. But I will... I promise."

I wipe my face, the tears caking the dirt to my cheeks, and suck in a settling breath. "You better," I say, gathering my crutches, and I turn for the graveyard without waiting for his reply. "Or I'm breaking your other nose."

"His other nose?" Jacks says as I pass them.

"Whatever," I huff. I can't think straight. "I'll break it again."

We stay back to give Jacks some time alone at his mother's grave. Arms crossed, Riddick and Cole stand on one side of me, Luxxe on the other. Nobody's speaking.

Rain starts to fall in soft sheets, misting our faces and shoulders. It won't be long before the bottom falls out.

Jacks' back is to us, his shoulders heaving with sobs. The image tears my heart in two every time – Jacks, so frail and helpless, mourning over the one parent he had left.

It's not fair.

I'm thankful he has a place to mourn in remembrance, though. There's a sense of closure in that, I would guess. If only a little. I was never granted the opportunity to see my parents' bodies or know where they were taken. The only hope I have of closure is to pretend they're somewhere like this – a quaint little cemetery shaded by weeping willows. I imagine a bouquet of peace lilies, my mother's favorite flowers, draped across a headstone that reads, "In loving memory of a beautiful soul." My father's reads, "A man who loved with all his heart lies here." Sometimes it helps me... when I allow my thoughts to wander there.

My eyes skim the cemetery. So much heartache packed into one tiny nook of the island. So many needless deaths. There must be hundreds of wooden crosses now. Most of them were here within six

Spectacle

months of our arrival. The sick and the elderly didn't stand a chance. Then winter came, which isn't harsh here, but one can still get hypothermia if they don't keep warm enough. Not to mention, snake bites. The rest were laid to rest because of pneumonia, asthma attacks, allergic reactions. Things we could have cured with access to modern medicine. Our holistic doctor is good, but there are some things he can't treat.

Jacks motions to me, and I start his way on one crutch, my other arm cradling the flowers, so I can leave them on her grave. I often wonder what I would put on Tabitha's headstone. Probably "Tabitha, a breakable body but an unbreakable will." I attribute a lot of who I am to her. She's part of the reason I'm so strong. She took me in when I was parentless and taught me more than just gardening and survival, she taught me how to carry on despite the chaos and hopelessness around us. Her and Maggie both, and I have a terrible feeling I'll be exercising those teachings in the days to come.

Glassy-eyed, I settle beside him. He reaches for my hand with a grateful smile. He likes for me to sit with him and share memories of her before we leave. I always begin our visit by reciting Frost's *Reluctance*. He says it soothes him.

As I stammer through the first verse, I can't help but wonder what Tabitha would say about Luxxe's decision to volunteer. She was always the voice of reason. But, honestly, nothing comes to mind. Is there ever a good reason to leave your friends and family behind when the rest of the world has already left them for dead?

Chapter 17

I watch Jacks as he sleeps by the candlelight. Days like today always take a lot out of him – physically and emotionally.

After I joined him at the gravesite, we only had a few minutes to reminisce before the rain poured, drenching all of us to the bone. Lightning followed. Cole offered to carry Jacks back to our cabin to give Riddick a break, and Riddick agreed, so he and Luxxe made their way to camp. Cole left shortly after we arrived. Begrudgingly. He insisted he stay to help with dinner and anything else we needed, but today took a lot out of me too, and I just wanted to get it all done and settle in for the night. I also wasn't up for any more company.

The storm didn't let up for hours, but it's silent now, save the residual raindrops rolling from leaf to leaf as they make their way down to the earth. When a breeze rolls through, the raindrops scurry faster in waves, and the soft, transient noise reminds me of the ocean and the times Luxxe and I would steal away to the cliffs. When we were younger, he used to come wake me on clear nights with a full moon, and we'd stay there until sunrise, eating blackberries and pretending we were somewhere else, anywhere else but this island.

We haven't been back since Tabitha passed.

Distracting myself from those memories, I move my attention to wrapping my knee with a fresh bandage. I still can't comprehend how that boy, the one I'd grown up with, shared my secrets and fears and hopes with, could think of leaving us. He'd better follow through with his promise and explain everything the first chance he gets. I can only imagine the earful Maggie's giving him now. Rightfully so. I'd also kill to know how Taylor feels about it all; though I'm sure she's devastated like the rest of us.

Luxxe's voice rolls through with the wind. "*Mira...*" he whispers, like he used to do when he'd come for me during the night.

I follow his voice to the door, his body filling the frame. He moves quietly inside. Maggie follows.

"What are you doing here?" I ask. I figured they'd be tucked inside their huts by now. It's too wet for a bonfire tonight.

"How's that knee?" he asks, his voice low and urgent. The candlelight flickers across his features, and his brow is furrowed, his eyes severe with a trace of caution. He's on a mission.

I eye him skeptically. "Okay, I guess."

"Good enough for a walk?"

I look to Maggie. She, too, wears a look of guarded urgency, but she also looks spooked, like she's facing some twisted, horrible nightmare. Except she is; her son wants to leave us. And, unfortunately, it's not a dream. "I... I guess so. Let me get my crutches."

"On second thought," he says, scooping me into his arms before I can blink, "We need to move quickly. I'll carry you."

I don't argue.

We're already on our way down the path before I realize what's going on. "So, is *this* the part where you explain everything?" I smack his chest for emphasis.

"Would you quit with the abuse?" he scolds.

"That's nothing compared to what you've put me through today," I counter.

He winces at the thought, his features softening. "I know. I'm sorry."

"Well?"

"Well, what?"

"Is this where you tell me?"

"Almost," he says. "Things will be explained when we get there."

"There?"

"Yes... That's why we're moving quickly. We need to work everything out and have everyone back before sunrise."

I cock my head at him. Work everything out? *Everyone?*

"So, nobody at camp knows we've been gone," he explains.

"You're not making sense, Luxxe."

"Blythe will tell you everything you need to know."

Wait... *what?* "What does Blythe have to do with today?"

"More than you'd think."

I grit my teeth, this talking-in-code thing pissing me off. "Just tell me!"

He sighs. "Have some patience, please..."

Ha. He's one to talk. I scowl at him, making sure he sees it before turning my face away. At least I'm getting close to an explanation. If I don't kill him first.

Luxxe takes me down the path toward camp, but before we arrive, he slips onto another path I've never seen. This one is crooked and narrow, and branches graze against my jeans as we walk, soaking them in rainwater. The moon still hides behind the clouds, so I can't see a thing, but I know Luxxe can see well enough to get us where we're going. Changers are supposed to have better night vision than humans, though I apparently didn't inherit the trait. I can't see anything without some kind of light to guide me. Maybe when I get my markings. *If* I get them. I'm beginning to think it won't happen. Maybe half-breeds like me don't get them. Since I'm the only half-breed in our tribe, there's no sure way to know. Although, I've never seen any older Changers at Commencement Day without them, so maybe there's hope. But, hey... at least I have some freakish knack for teleporting without meaning to.

The path goes on forever. I'm certain we've been walking for the better part of an hour. "How much longer?" I ask, nestling into him. Not because I've forgiven him yet or am trying to show him any kind of affection. The storm brought cooler temperatures – at least ten degrees – and Luxxe radiates heat like an oven. Must be all that hot air.

"We have a while," he replies, his voice stiff and distant. His mind is elsewhere again.

I try to read his expression through the dark but can't. I'd give anything to know what's going on inside that head of his. What's in store for me when we get wherever we're going? What's in store for *him*, and why Blythe or anyone else has something to do with it? I think of the look on Maggie's face and swallow over the lump in my throat.

"What?" he asks. I'm sure he sees me squinting at him.

"Nothing," I lie.

"You still mad at me?" he asks after a short pause.

"Furious."

"Thought so," he mumbles. "Sorry."

"You better be," I say, trying to sound stern, except my voice quivers. I might be mad. I might be hurt. But I'm also scared. I don't want him to get chosen. I don't want to lose him. I don't want to live the rest of my life wondering what his fate was.

He gives me a gentle squeeze.

"Sorry about your nose, though," I add.

"It's fine. Sorry about your forehead. Does it hurt?"

I run my fingertips over the scab. "I'll live."

We break into a pasture, skirt around a pond, and enter the woods again. The trail takes a hard right, then a subtle incline. This one's a little wider and gives my legs a break from the constant brushing. My pants are so soaked now the moisture is running into my boots.

The next time we exit the woods, I gasp, blinking feverishly against the darkness to make sure I'm seeing right. The skeletal remains of a town long forgotten fracture the horizon, and it fills me with an odd mixture of nostalgia and unease. I haven't seen buildings in years. "What is this place?" I ask.

"Some old town," he replies. "We don't know the name, though. Nobody's found a sign."

We get closer, and from what little moonlight filters through the clouds, I make out crumbling brick walls and square-shaped holes where windows used to be. His feet patter against the remnants of a paved road leading toward them, but so many weeds have punctured through you'd never know it was here until you stepped on it, the asphalt claimed by the willowy army of plants.

"You think this town was pre-Great Disaster?" I ask.

"Looks that way. The only things they've found are skeletons and rusted cars."

"Guess none of them made it through the earthquakes?"

"That's my guess."

I stare at the storefronts as we pass through. They remind me of the buildings Jacks and I passed every day on the way home – small-town stores. I imagined one was a pharmacy, one a market and one a bank. A clothing store. A pet store. Restaurant. Places that used to teem with life and vibrancy and were now the decaying bits and pieces of a nameless society.

When we arrived six years ago, the adults figured the island was once a piece of land that had broken away from somewhere in the East during the Great Disaster. Pine and maple trees aren't the norm for islands. At least the islands before the earth changed. They told us the old islands with palm trees and sandy beaches are submerged like everything else. Something no one will probably ever see again.

"Not much further," he assures me, and nods toward the last building on this block. Lights from inside glow radiantly against the night.

"Okay," I say breathlessly, knowing once we arrive I'll finally have the answers I want, and I'm not sure whether I'm relieved or scared shitless.

Spectacle

Chapter 18

Inside the dilapidated building, we enter a room on the left, the light from inside washing over us. It takes a moment for my eyes to adjust. The room is cavernous with cracked concrete floors, high walls, and exposed steel pipes. Part of the roof has rotted away along the back wall, leaving the floor wet with a musty smell to the air. At the room's center is a makeshift table with scrap pieces of wood and cinderblocks for a base. A map sprawls across its surface; Blythe is poring over it by the light of two lanterns. She's wearing glasses, her concentrated stare etching hard lines in her face and aging her well beyond her years. Taylor and Jonah stand over her on one side, and an older man – I'm guessing in his seventies – sits on the other on an overturned plastic bucket. He's explaining whatever Blythe is studying so intensely. Behind them stands Riddick, his mom, Cole, and someone I haven't met before. Judging by the bone jewelry adorning his wrists and neck, I'm assuming he belongs to the desert tribe. Everyone looks worse for wear – frazzled and worried and sad. Except Blythe. She looks determined.

"We're here," Luxxe announces. His voice ricochets off the walls. Everyone looks to us.

"Come," Blythe says, pulling a weathered, plastic chair to the table, "Let her sit here."

Luxxe carries me to the chair and gingerly sets me into it. It could be my imagination, but I swear a spark of jealousy ignites in Taylor's eyes as she watches. I *have* taken up a lot of his time the past two days, after all. She'll get over it.

Once the warmth of his arms leaves me, I curl into myself on the chair, bringing my knees to my chest and wrapping my arms around them. I feel so vulnerable in this huge, moldy room with the threat of something dire hanging in the air. I don't like feeling vulnerable.

As if sensing it, the old man attempts to give me a comforting smile, the corners of his thin lips disappearing into his wrinkles. I nod my hello, noting I've seen him at the market a time or two, though I don't know his name. He's completely bald, his spotted head reminding me of a robin's egg, and he wears a beaded necklace with boar tusks dangling in the center. His eyes always sparkle as though his soul is years younger than its aging vessel.

Riddick's mom, Jennie, scoots another bucket between me and the old man, and Blythe settles onto it, her focused but tired eyes searching mine. She manages a smile, her hand moving to the wooden pendant around her neck with our symbol on it. She rubs her thumb over the etching. "How are you, Mira?" she asks. The silver in her dreads shimmers in the light. She's only in her forties, but I imagine the stress of looking after a flock of people could give one plenty of grey hairs.

I try to speak confidently. "I'm good." Minus the dreaded feeling in every facet of my soul that my world is about to be permanently turned upside down. It kind of already has.

Her eyes flicker up to the scab on my forehead, but she doesn't say anything. "And your knee?" she asks.

"Still sprained."

"She tried to run on it earlier," Cole explains.

Blythe doesn't seem surprised. Her hand clasps my forearm for a moment with a tender squeeze. "Always strong," she says approvingly. "But you have to take care of yourself too."

Cole and Luxxe nod in agreement.

I smile weakly, and I release my legs, my feet squishing in my water-soaked socks as my boots rest against the floor. Anyone else besides an Elder would have gotten an eye roll. I don't know her that well, but Maggie tells me she asks about me and Jacks often; it's her duty to keep tabs on everyone in camp. But I can tell it's more than that. She genuinely cares.

Luxxe kneels on the other side of me at the table, his bulging arms resting against its edge. He eyes me warily, concern and a deep, festering worry eating him from the inside. Blythe removes her glasses, rubs her temples as is to relieve an aching pressure, and then refocuses on me. "I'm sure you want to know what's going on," she says.

I swallow hard and nod.

"Then I'll cut to the chase, but before I do, I expect whatever is said in this room to stay here."

I nod again. "I promise."

Her eyes search mine. For what, I don't know. Maybe for a sign I can handle whatever she's about to tell me. She continues anyway. "I'm part of a movement..." She pauses and points to everyone in the room. "...*we're* all part of a movement to bring President Howell and his conspirators to justice. This includes the lowlifes at FM Incorporated."

I look to Luxxe and he gives me an affirming nod.

Blythe continues. "We have proof that President Howell put us here to not only improve the overpopulation issue but to also improve the economy with the creation of the Freedom Matches."

She gives me a second to let that sink in, then says, "As you know, we were never a threat to the human race. It was all made up to get us here. And your father." She nods in Luxxe's direction. "And *his* father were chess pieces in the entire game. We know your father

Spectacle

didn't start the shooting that day at the White House. They were..." she considers her next words.

"Executed," the old man supplies.

I flinch.

"Executed," Blythe repeats softly. "And then blamed for the shooting to make the humans hate and fear us even more than they already did. President Howell needed pawns to get the ball rolling and your fathers were perfect targets."

A supportive hand clamps to my shoulder. The zig-zag markings tell me it's Cole. Luxxe grabs for my hand.

"Should I continue?" Blythe asks, searching my eyes again.

I nod, and I hope it's as confidently as I intended. None of what she's saying surprises me at all, but I know she's just grazing the surface of why they really brought me here. Luxxe gives my hand a squeeze.

"The reason we know this for sure is because there's a recording of Vice President Wu and a board member at FM Incorporated, before FM Incorporated even got its licensing, bragging how they'd set up your fathers, how they'd arranged for our transportation here before the 'attack' at the White House even happened, and how the matches were going to be structured. And just as importantly, how much money the government would get for helping arrange all of this... in the form of a lump sum. Not to mention the annual taxes from profits and ticket sales and merchandise."

She pauses again, giving me a moment to process. Images flash through my mind - gunfire at the White House. The hospital. My mourning mother. The men in uniform killing her and taking me away. The cemetery and all the lives lost over the past six years. Despite the nausea and revulsion churning inside me, I nod for her to keep going.

"And we believe all of this – improving the population issues and economy – was not just about the money, it was also in hopes of keeping all of them in office."

The old man releases a disgusted snort. Jonah echoes with one of his own. I notice he hasn't made an attempt to add anything yet. Blythe must be running the show.

"They're up for re-election in two years, and we believe if the humans, the public, knew about this, they'd be outraged. Now, they believe we're dangerous, but if they found out what really happened, what the truth is, they'd call for impeachments of Howell and Wu and new candidates would be voted in. And FM would be done for."

The old man butts in. "And then we'd have a chance at going back home," he says. "Those of us who want to stay could stay. But those of us who want to go back could go back."

Blythe gives him a hopeful look. "That's the plan - shed light. Bring justice." She looks back to me, something infectious burning in her eyes. "Give us true freedom."

"Not the kind that has to be earned through bloodshed," Luxxe adds.

I scowl at him. Speaking of... "So where does you volunteering to fight fit in?"

"Well..." Blythe says, answering for him. "...it's part of our plan. We know the recording exists, but they need help getting to it."

I give her a puzzled look.

"And 'they' are my brother and those working with him."

Brother? "I didn't know you had..."

"He's not a Changer. Technically, he's my brother-in-law, though I've always called him my brother. We were... *are*... very close. I married into a human family not long after our kind arrived here on Earth." Her eyes take on a darker shade of sadness, and she has to wait a minute before continuing. I heard her husband was injured and thrown in jail for trying to fight off the soldiers when they came for her. "It's a long story. One I'll tell you someday when we have more time." She shifts in her seat and presses her eyes shut, preparing herself for another long explanation. How many times has she gone through what she's about to tell me? My eyes drift over the others in the room and up to Cole standing behind me, his hand still on my shoulder. He gives me a ghost of a smile.

Luxxe squeezes my hand again, and I ignore Taylor's glare.

"This recording," she begins. "I'm sure you're wondering how we know it exists. How we know any of this."

Spectacle

I nod. We're cut off from New America. No phones. No computers. No anything.

"My brother is pretty high up in the military — a senior officer. And before they shipped us away, he came to me and told me he had his suspicions that something was going on and we needed to go into hiding. Of course, it wasn't in time. And there was nothing he could do once the orders were given. He tried to find us and hide us himself, but they'd already gotten us on the boat and on the way here.

"But since the Freedom Matches began, he's used a trusted friend on FM guard duty to slip me notes on Commencement Day. So that's how we've been communicating — the guard slips me notes, and I slip him mine to give to my brother."

Clever.

"His first note explained that another friend of his gave him a copy of the recording. Someone he grew up with who served as a detective on the police force for many years, and then later went into business for himself as a private detective. That's how he was able to get the recording of Wu and the FM board member."

"He bugged the board member's phone line," the old man says, smirking, as though he personally bugged the phone line himself.

"His wife suspected him of cheating," Blythe explains. "She'd hired the detective to find out for sure."

"And then he happened to hear things he shouldn't have."

I gently clear my throat, and Blythe pauses, waiting for what I have to say. "So why doesn't the detective testify? Or take the recording to a news station?"

"Remember when I said they need help getting to it?" she asks.

Oh yeah.

"That *was* the plan," the old man says. "To expose them. But something told the detective to make a copy and give it to her brother, just in case."

"And good thing he did," she adds. "Somehow, the husband found out about the detective spying on him, and not even a day later, the detective came up missing and his office mysteriously burned to the ground."

Oh my God.

"After that, my brother decided to hide the copy of their conversation somewhere safe. Somewhere nobody would ever suspect until he could decide what to do with it. He knew he needed a careful plan. Something well thought out and meticulous. He didn't want anyone else he knew 'disappearing' because of it."

"He should know where it's at," I say.

Blythe smiles, but it's weary and brittle. "Yes, we know where it's at. But they need help getting to it."

I frown, confused.

"Let them finish," Luxxe whispers.

"So, my brother decided the best place to hide it was the one place Howell and Wu wouldn't expect – the White House. He told nobody. Just tucks it away on the twelfth floor, which has rooms completely dedicated to storing classified records."

"Genius, if you ask me," the old man says. "Hide it under their noses."

Luxxe gives an approving grunt.

"The only problem is," Blythe continues. "Shortly after, they put the twelfth floor on lockdown and it's been that way ever since."

"Seems they might have other things they want to protect," the old man adds.

"I have no doubt," Blythe agrees.

"Your brother can't get back in there?" I ask.

"Unfortunately, not. Only Howell, Wu, and their personal administrators have clearance."

Convenient.

"But that's not to say it's impossible. We just have to use other... *creative* methods." She turns her attention to the map. "My brother has a plan to blow the lid off this entire thing now; he just needs to get his hands on the recording again to see it through."

I glance over the fine, charcoal-colored lines on the paper. An intricate maze with fat pathways winding and intersecting with smaller ones. Tubes of some kind? Pipes, maybe? Nothing I've seen before.

Spectacle

"And that's where we come in," the old man says. His smile is diabolical now. "We're going to help him break in."

Chapter 19

"Why does he need *our* help?" I ask. We're miles and miles away, surrounded by ocean. How could we possibly help him at all? It then dawns on me that, if chosen, Luxxe will be traveling back to New America in two weeks. A ferocious dread knots my stomach. Has he volunteered for way more than a bloody fight in a Freedom Match? My gut tells me yes.

Blythe shifts on her bucket. The puffiness rimming her eyes tells me she hasn't slept well in days. "Because the twelfth floor, and the floors above and below it, are heavily guarded now. He couldn't simply try and sneak in without raising suspicion. He needs a different way in."

I instinctually look to the map again.

"And this," the old man says, sweeping his hand across it, "is his way in."

Spectacle

"My brother tried to find the plans for the building in hopes he might be able to use the air ducts or some well-hidden pathway to get to the room, but he didn't have any luck. The building had been renovated by an architectural firm about twenty years ago, so he was hoping they should still have the plans somewhere. But guess what happened when he visited the firm to find them?"

I didn't want to guess, my imagination conjuring all kinds of horrible things. And apparently, the government was capable of all of them.

"They didn't have them," the old man answers for me.

"What if they were lying?" I ask.

"They weren't. And I know because I was the architect." The sparkle in his eyes dulls a little. "The government asked for the plans as soon as I finished the project."

"Why?"

"Guess they didn't want anyone to have access to them." He shrugs. "Made sense, at the time, to me. Why would they want anyone else to have intimate knowledge of their building?"

Blythe heaves a sigh. "The plans, I'm sure, are on the twelfth floor as well. With everything else we need." She turns her attention to the old man, patting his shoulder lovingly. "But thankfully, Harvey here has an excellent memory."

My attention snaps back to the table. "The plans..." I whisper, and hope rouses inside me. He recreated them.

"Yes," Harvey says. "I was able to redraw the plans. Now we need to get them to him."

"That's part of the reason my brother contacted us," Blythe explains. "He knew Harvey was sent here. When he went looking for the plans, they told him he was shipped off to the island with the rest of the Changers."

"He was hoping I was still alive," the old man says. His lips twist into a smirk, the youthful sparkle reigniting in his eyes. "It'll take more than a boat ride and an island to kill this old man."

Everyone chuckles gravely.

I look back to Luxxe. "And you're the one taking them to him."

Luxxe offers me an apologetic half-smile and shrugs.

"Smart girl," Blythe says.

The words fly out without my permission. "*No.* Someone else can do it."

The room falls silent for a moment, minus the pinging of stray moths bumping against the glass of the lanterns.

"It's already been done," she explains quietly. "I'm sorry."

"Then we need to undo it."

I pull my hand from Luxxe's, twist my shoulder from Cole's grip.

"I'm afraid I can't."

The old man flashes another sympathetic smile.

"Why?"

"Because Luxxe has already volunteered, and people are working to get him chosen as we speak. It's done."

"Well, undo it!"

"Mira..." Luxxe chides. I shouldn't raise my voice at an Elder.

"Sorry," I say, but the resentment in my voice is still apparent. "I just... Can't anyone else do this? What about one of the other volunteers?"

Blythe holds a confident, unyielding expression, but her eyes and voice soften. "My brother wants someone from our tribe because he trusts me. And he asked me to approach only those *I* trust with this information. We need a believable volunteer." Her eyes drift to Luxxe, and they shimmer with tears. "And Luxxe was the best candidate Harvey and I could think of."

I continue watching her as she looks at him, and I realize as much as she's steadfast and unwavering in her resolve to see this mission through, she hates the idea of Luxxe going as much as I do. Except there is a difference – she's allowing it to happen. I would never put him in danger like this. I wouldn't even consider it. I love him more than that.

My gaze moves to Riddick, then Cole, and for a split second, I consider suggesting why not them. They are capable and strong. But then I also realize I wouldn't want that to happen either. I hang my head. What a mess.

"You okay?" she asks.

I don't answer. Of course, I'm not okay.

Spectacle

"The fight will be fixed, as well," Luxxe adds, as if it's supposed to soothe me. It only makes me bristle.

"And what if, somehow, the wrong person finds out about this plan?" I say sharply. "Then what? You'll be dead in minutes... or *missing*. Like the detective."

"It'll be fine."

I bark out a frustrated laugh. "How could you even know that?"

"My brother will keep him safe," Blythe assures me.

"If they don't kill him too."

"This plan will work," she shoots back. "We're not saying it's without risks, but sometimes, we have to take chances for the greater good."

"Think of what this could mean," the old man says. "Think about what this could accomplish. We can clear your fathers' names. Bring justice."

"And we can be a part of that," Luxxe echoes.

I let out a long breath, but it does little to calm me. Cole reaches for my shoulder again, but I wrench away. "And what do you think your father would say about this if he were still alive?" I ask Luxxe. "What does Maggie say?"

Luxxe deflates a little. "She's mad," he admits. "And scared."

You *think?*

"But she also knows there's no changing my mind. I want to do this. It's not like they're forcing me."

I fight the urge to glare at Blythe. If she'd never approached him about their plans, none of this would have happened. Now I'm losing my friend. By death or victory at the Freedom Match, he's still leaving us. "Say you win and everything goes right. Then what?"

"It's hard to say," the old man answers for him. "Our hope is things will change and those of us who want to travel back, can."

"And I'll come back," Luxxe says. "I wouldn't leave my mom like that."

"And *me*," I say. "And Taylor and Jacks and Cole and Riddick and-"

"That's the other thing," Luxxe sighs. He looks at me hesitantly.

I stare back. What now?

He presses his lips, gathering courage. "As a chosen volunteer, I'll get to take three people with me."

So?

"To help me train and for moral support. And whether I win or lose, my team will be brought back here to the island."

"But the Match will be fixed for him to win," Blythe reminds me. "And really, you would just be there for show. Since everything's fixed and we're only using you guys to transfer the plans. This should all be easy."

"A piece of cake," the old man agrees.

I'm staring at her now. She said, 'you guys.' Why would she say, 'you guys?'

"We're hoping you'll go with us," Luxxe explains.

I...

Did I hear him right? "Excuse me?" I whisper.

"We're hoping-"

"No, I heard what you said. I just..."

Luxxe smiles nervously. "I want you to be one of my three."

Tingles shoot up my spine and out my arms. Heat floods my cheeks. "Right," I say, and hobble to my feet, my boots making a squishy sound. I've heard enough.

Blythe looks confused, and Luxxe stands to help me. "Don't..." I seethe. "Don't you touch me."

"Mira, I-"

"How *could* you?" I say. "It's one thing to volunteer yourself for something like this, but how could you even consider asking me to go? You know I can't leave Jacks. Why would you ask me to?"

"My mom will stay with him while we're gone. She's already agreed to it."

"You already *asked* her?" I'm seeing red now, my voice and entire body shaking. "That's not your place. I haven't agreed to go!"

He doesn't reply.

"What if something *does* happen to us, Luxxe? Then he's lost more people he's counting on." Tears sting my eyes, and I say the rest through a tight throat. "I'm his support now. I won't leave him."

"I-"

Spectacle

"Take me back," I demand, and I turn to Blythe, swiping away a tear. "I'm sorry. Good luck with all this, but I can't be a part of it. I'm needed here."

She nods, her eyes filled with compassion. "I understand," she says, and I believe she truly does; she knows what it's like to have people depending on her. Except, I wouldn't ask her to think of leaving them.

Luxxe sweeps me into his arms.

"Get her back safely," Blythe says, and we turn for the door. I ignore the eyes on our backs as we leave, not wasting a single thought as to what everyone's thinking about my outburst. I don't care. I'm not participating in any of this. I'm not leaving Jacks. I'm not.

Chapter 20

We reach the pond in the clearing before I speak to Luxxe again. I've had enough time to let everything sink in and decide where I want to start. "What are you thinking, Luxxe?" I mumble, absently rubbing my pendant. I'm not mad anymore, just confused and broken.

His chest heaves against me as he sighs. "Which part?"

"All of it. But let's start with you volunteering, again."

"They need me to do something important. I accepted."

"Did you ever consider what this would do to all of us if this goes wrong? If something happens to you, we'll all be devastated."

He slows to a stop. I can barely see his eyes in the darkness, but their intensity is palpable. "Every minute since Blythe came to me with this."

I pause for a beat. "Then why?"

Spectacle

"Because, sometimes, there are things bigger than us in life. Sometimes, we have to do what's right, even if it means risking everything."

Spoken like a true warrior. "This is what you wanted to tell me yesterday, isn't it? Before the hunt?"

"It killed me not to."

"I know."

The silence we stand in is eaten away by the chorus of singing frogs, then he says, "I really am sorry this is hurting you."

I nod somberly.

"But do you see my side in this at all?"

I take a moment to consider my answer. Do I understand the importance of what this mission could mean? Of course. It means retribution. It means true freedom. It means truth will reign where nothing but deceit and death have ruled for years. But where my understanding wavers is the part where my best friend wants to risk his life for it all. It's a noble thought, I admit, but I want him around. Call me selfish. "I'm not sure yet," I reply.

He continues into the darkness.

"But you could have told me, ya know. Why didn't you?"

"I know. But Blythe made me swear I wouldn't say anything until tonight."

I glare at her in my thoughts. As much as I respect her, she isn't my favorite person right now.

"Otherwise I would have told you right away," he assures me, and I know he's telling the truth. We don't keep secrets from each other. Usually.

"And this whole the-fight-will-be-fixed thing. You know that for sure?"

"Blythe's brother assured us it would be. He has people on the inside at FM. They're going to make it happen."

My anxiety eases at the idea. Only slightly. I'll still be mad with worry when he leaves.

"And sorry if you feel like I was trying to drag you through all this. Part of me thought you'd want to be a part of the movement that'll help bring our fathers justice."

Inexplicably, guilt stabs into me. Should I feel more driven to clear my father's name? He was *executed*, then made out to be the villain. Still, something tells me he wouldn't approve. "Not sure my dad would want me to be involved in this."

Luxxe says nothing, so I know he agrees. My dad wouldn't want me to endanger myself in any way. Though, I can't help but wonder if somewhere deep inside that disapproval, if I ever chose to help with this mission, if he'd be proud that I was being brave and bold like Luxxe. Or maybe it's stupid and careless. I guess courage can be seen as all those things, depending on the lens you're viewing it through.

Not that it matters. I'm not leaving Jacks.

"And I'm guessing all of this is why you looked like you wanted to vomit yesterday?" I ask, to change the subject. I didn't want him to think I was entertaining the idea of going with him to New America... in case I didn't make myself clear enough back at the building.

"What?"

"When you saw the cameras yesterday, you totally looked like you wanted to hurl."

He hesitates. "No, I didn't."

"You *so* did..."

He sighs through his nose. "Okay, maybe the thought of being on camera..."

"Scared you a little?" I hope he sees my smirk.

"Not *scared*," he says, a little too defensively.

"Then what?"

He's quiet again. *Uh huh.*

"Shut up," he snaps.

I can't help but chuckle. "You better get used to it since they're fixing the vote," I say, and all the humor leaves my voice. The thought of him flying away in a helicopter stabs me in the heart again.

"I know," he says flatly. "Madden told me I'll be on camera a lot."

"Madden?"

"Oh, yeah. You wanted to leave before we could introduce you."

I think back to the building. "The desert tribe guy?"

Spectacle

"Yeah. Blythe summoned for him this morning. She asked the Elder there to send one of their last volunteers' team members, so they sent Madden. He went with Emerson six months ago."

I want to ask if Madden mentioned the outcome of that battle but decide against it. I don't want to know. "I'm assuming she wanted you to know what to expect once they come and get you?"

"Yeah. And go ahead and assemble a team. Usually, the team is picked the day they come and get us, according to Madden. Which I'm thankful for, really. Until we met with him tonight, we assumed I'd be going alone."

"Cause nobody from our tribe has ever gone," I add. "Who's going with you, then?" I ask, though I don't really want to know that either.

"Since you're out, now, it'll be Taylor, Cole, and Riddick."

I'm nauseous again. So, basically, everyone I'm close to now is putting their life on the line. But wait... "What do you mean *because I'm out now*?"

"Cole and Taylor were going either way, but Riddick was prepared to go if you didn't."

I blanch, thinking of what his mother must be going through because I declined. The nausea worsens.

"You okay?"

Why does everyone keep asking me that? Of course, I'm not okay! I swallow the bile down. "No, I'm not okay," I snap. On top of everything else, now I feel a staggering sense of guilt.

"Dumb question. Sorry."

I scoff, then I want to cry. I bury my face in my hands.

He hugs me to him. "Want to go to our spot tonight?" he asks, almost whispers.

The thought fills me with equal amounts of warmth and icy bitterness. Ironic how, now that he's leaving and the future's unknown, all of a sudden, he wants unadulterated friend-time with me. We haven't had that in years. Not really. Not without a reason like training or hunting or helping me with Jacks. "For a little," I say, knowing if I decline, and something happens to him after all of this is said and done, I'll regret it forever.

When we make it to the main path headed for camp, he takes a left.

Chapter 21

"Thank you for not pressuring me to go," I say, popping a blackberry in my mouth. They're more tart than they used to be, but still delicious. The burst of flavor brings back so many memories.

"I'd never do that," he says, draping a muscular arm around my shoulders. "This isn't a decision someone should be guilted into. That's why I waited to tell you about Riddick being your alternate until after you made your decision."

I nod, nestling into him... my sweet, cranky, stupidly heroic friend. "Well, thank you, anyway... *Solomon*."

He half grunts, half laughs. "Yeah, I didn't want to give them my other name."

"Luxxe sounds meaner, though," I note, then jab him with my elbow. "Fits you better."

"Actually, Blythe insisted I use a different name. She said since my dad was one of the ones that supposedly started the war, the officials probably know my name. Luxxe isn't necessarily a name you'd forget."

I nod my agreement.

"And she didn't want to risk me not being chosen. Even if her brother-in-law is rigging it from the inside, I doubt the President would knowingly allow any of us back into New America."

"But what if they recognize you?"

"I have blue marks and dreads now. I don't think that'll be an issue."

True. "So, what would my name have been?" I muse. Mirabella isn't a common name, either.

"Oh, you wouldn't have mattered," he says, jabbing me back, "I'll be the star of the show. They don't ask for your names."

I roll my eyes. He'll end up liking this whole thing more than he should. He's never minded being the center of attention. When cameras aren't involved, anyway.

The inky black ocean arrests our attention. The clouds have parted, the moon and starlight glittering against its surface. Out of habit, I check to see if the moon has any rings around it, and it doesn't. The last time I saw them was the night before Tabitha was bitten. I'll check it every night Luxxe and my friends are away from here.

I close my eyes and will the moment and briny ocean air to calm me, though it's mostly futile. A word still rings through my subconscious unbidden – *executed*. I thought knowing what truly happened to my father might bring relief, but if anything, it's only rubbed salt in my wounds. I knew he must have died from gunfire, but the word "executed" conjures so many uncomfortable images.

"Do you forgive me?" he asks. "I can't leave knowing you hate me for any of this."

"Don't get ahead of yourself," I say, mostly joking. "But you're my friend. You always will be."

"I'll take it," he says, planting a kiss on my hair.

Spectacle

We sit like this until dawn casts an orangey-pink sheen on the water.

When we get back to the cabin, Maggie is asleep on my mat, a half-empty bottle of blackberry wine clutched in her hand. Riddick's mom must have armed her with a bottle. Jennie – a former distillery worker – is our camp's booze maker. Luxxe and I sigh in tandem. Maggie only drinks when she's stressed to her absolute limit.

"When I leave, it's going to kill her, isn't it?" he whispers, setting me on a stool in the kitchen. I get to work on unlacing my soggy boots.

"It already is," I reply, and think, *you're all she truly has left*, but I decide to keep that to myself. The pained look on his face tells me he already knows it.

Speaking of moms, I think of Riddick's again, but close my eyes to fling it away. *Not my fault*. Riddick can always bow out if he wants, though I know he won't. He's too much like Luxxe and Cole... except for his fear of bushy-tailed rodents. But it's not my problem. It can't be. I look to Jacks. This is where my responsibilities lie. Here, in this home. With my friend who needs me. Our time is already shadowed by the promise that his disease will slowly but surely claim his life. Time is precious as it is. I don't want to spend more time away from him than I have to.

"You know," Luxxe says, crouching to meet my eyes, "I said I didn't want to guilt you, and I meant it, but I want you to know the thought of having you with me in New America helped give me courage this morning."

My stomach drops as I pull my boots and socks off.

"You're one of the bravest people I know," he says and kisses my hair one last time. As I watch him leave, I realize that, even though I've decided to stay, maybe Luxxe needs me as much as Jacks. The only difference is, one of them is choosing their fate while the other is a victim of theirs. And while my heart is with them both, I can't be two places at once. I've made my choice.

Doesn't make it hurt any less, though.

A piece of me will leave with Luxxe in two weeks and I may never get it back. Tears fill my eyes at the thought, and the urge to hobble after him and plead with him not to go overcomes me. To stay here and just live our lives and forget everything we've been told. But I don't, because I also know that would be asking him to compromise himself and what he feels he needs to do. I can't ask that of him. I want to, but I can't. I'll have to live with it.

"Morning," a sleepy voice says.

"Morning," I say, smiling a teary smile at Jacks. Yes, I definitely made the right decision.

I watch as Jack sips the broth I warmed from our stew last night and wait with a cloth to dab any dribbles. My eyes roam over him, all the way from his rumpled dark hair to his toes, making sure he didn't get any bug bites during the night – not an unusual occurrence in the summer. They stop on his left eye. A shadow of blue rims the outer corner. "Did you fall last night?" I ask, gingerly removing his glasses.

"No," he replies. "Why?"

I lean closer, a smile twitching on my lips. That isn't a bruise. "Jacks..."

He mirrors my enthusiastic grin. "What?"

"Your markings are coming in."

He's glowing now. "Really?"

"Yeah." I slide the glasses back on. "Pretty soon, you'll be able to change your skin."

He goes back to sipping, his hazel eyes distant as he revels in the idea. He's been waiting on his marks forever. A thought derails him, and his gaze snaps back to mine. He offers an apologetic wince. "Sorry," he says, and broth dribbles from the corner of his mouth. "Technically, you should have gotten yours first. You're older."

"Eh," I say dismissively, dabbing it before it runs down his neck, "I will eventually." *I think.*

"So...," he says, between sips. "You know what's going on now?" He gives me a smirk. "What do you think?"

I assess the knowing look on his face.

"Maggie told me everything last night after you left. I woke up."

"Well," I say, trying not to be irritated that she had already filled him in. I wanted to be the one to break the news. "I think Luxxe is crazy for doing it, but you know, as well as I, that he's going to do what he wants."

"Sounds familiar," he says pointedly.

"Shut up," I chuckle.

"Maggie's upset, though," he notes.

"I can imagine."

"But, ya know..." his eyes harden a little. "Can we really blame him? If I had a chance to get back at those bastards, I would."

I nod.

"If I were in better shape, I'd go with him."

I clasp his knee supportively. "I know. And I'm sure he'd want you there." *If only your body were as strong as your heart.*

"You going with him?"

I laugh. "No, Jacks. I'm not leaving you."

"You... you're not going?" he asks, and he seems confused by the notion.

I'm taken aback. "Did you want me to?"

We silently try to figure out the other. Our thoughts aren't usually this out of sync.

"I just figured you'd want to go," Jacks finally says. "I mean... this is big. *Really* big. We could clear our fathers' names."

I almost feel guilty now. And hurt. Does he not want me here? "I know, but I can't leave you, Jacks. What if something happens to me?"

"Something could happen to you here," he counters. "Look what happened to mom..."

I'm reeling. "You're saying you want me to go?"

"I'm saying you should consider it, at least."

I don't know what to say. All of this coming from the boy who worries every time I leave for a hunt. With good cause, too, apparently. I came back with a twisted knee.

Jacks shakily sets the bowl on the ground, then clasps my hand. "Don't look so hurt, Mira. You know I love you. You've been here for me when others probably would have run. It's not easy taking care of someone like me all the time."

I manage a smile. "Someone like you? You have the best attitude of anyone I've ever known."

"You know what I mean."

"I'm not leaving you, Jacks. You might be okay with it, but I won't even consider it."

He sighs. "What if I ask you to go on my behalf?"

I open my mouth to protest again, but he cuts me off. "No, really. I want this to happen. I want these assholes to pay."

I gape at him. I've never seen him this emboldened. "Aren't you at least concerned for me, though? What if things go wrong?"

He considers my words for a moment, then says, "But what if they don't? And you'll have Luxxe and Cole with you."

"But what if they *do*. We'll be outnumbered. It won't matter who's with me."

He sighs. "But what if they don't, Mira. What if we can fix all of this?" He looks away, takes another sip. "But if you don't want to," he says, shrugging, "I understand."

I laugh again, but not at him. It's more of a surprised, startled sound. "Are you... are you trying to manipulate me, Jackson Nathaniel?"

"Maybe," he says, fighting an impish grin, then his expression morphs into something more serious. "But don't you want this too? Don't you want these guys to pay?"

"Of course..."

"And you have to consider, if this goes as planned, that maybe I could go back to New America and have a better quality of life."

His words rail into me, and when I recover, I say, "Is what we have here so bad?"

Spectacle

He manages another smile. "No. But a wheelchair would be nice. And somewhere with air conditioning." He taps his broken lens. "New glasses."

I consider what he's saying, then nod in concession. Yes... it would. "*If* it goes to plan, though. And if we're allowed to move back. And even then, what if the humans are still violent toward us for a while? What if it's still not safe over there?"

"Would it kill you to think positive?" he says, and he tries to say it playfully but fails. It annoys him when I can't bring myself to.

I sigh. "Probably," I say jokingly.

He doesn't find it funny.

"I don't have to go for this to happen, though. You know that, right?"

He shrugs and picks up his bowl again. The fight in his eyes is fading. He knows I'm a lost cause when I've made up my mind... like another bullheaded person we know. "Just thought you'd want to, is all."

The borderline disappointment in his tone gives me a whole new sense of guilt, and I watch him sip his broth in puzzlement. How many ways can someone experience the same emotion? And in the same day? Broth dribbles down his chin again, and again, I dab it away. Resolution washes over me. He may not understand my position of wanting to stay here with him, but that's okay. It's the right thing to do.

Chapter 22

When Maggie pulls me outside after she wakes, stale wine and desperation oozing from her pores, I have a feeling what she's about to do – beg me to convince Luxxe to change his mind. I already have my reply on the tip of my tongue: I can't. This is his choice to make. But that isn't what she asks. "Please go," she whispers. Her eyes squint painfully against the morning sunlight.

"You too?" I breathe, leaning against a crutch.

"I heard you and Jacks," she admits. "And I'm with Jacks on this. I thought you'd want to go."

I throw a hand up, exasperated. The other one is grasping the crutch so hard it hurts.

"Don't be mad," she soothes. "It's not a bad thing; we think you're courageous."

"I'm also needed here," I say. "I'm not leaving him."

Spectacle

"I know," she concedes. "I know. But..." She checks to make sure Jacks hasn't tried to hobble closer to the door to listen, then lowers her voice. "You'll be an asset to the group."

I give her a look. *Really? Me?*

She bites her lip, contemplating her next words. She leans closer. "Don't be mad at him, but Luxxe told me about what happened the other day."

I wait for her to explain. I'm at a loss.

"On hunting day?"

My chin drops. *When I teleported.* "He told you?"

"He did. He was worried. But I'm glad he did."

"You are?"

"Yes... your dad would be too."

I cock my head. "He'd be worried or glad?"

"Both, I think... but mostly glad."

"How much wine have you had?"

She ignores me. "You know we were all from the same tribe, right? We've known each other for years."

"Yeah..."

"So, that means I knew your grandmother as well."

My heart swells. "You knew her?"

"Yes, dear. Only for a few years, but I knew her. You have her same light complexion and strong-willed personality." She tucks a stray hair behind my ear. "Her white-blonde hair."

I smile at the thought, then frown. "What does this have to do with what happened to me the other day?"

She pauses thoughtfully. "She could do the same thing."

I gasp, nearly choking. "What?"

"She called it space travel, I think. As in traveling through space matter. Not necessarily through outer space, though she could do that too." She looks at me concerned. "She said it was painful."

Remembering the searing burn before it happened, I wince. I guess the two are related. "She was right. But why would any of this make my dad happy?"

"He always suspected you took after her in more ways than one; he could never space travel like her. But he wanted to wait until your teenage years to really talk to you about it. That's when the ability is supposed to surface."

Looks that way. "And he was robbed of that opportunity," I added for her.

"Most definitely."

"So, what was she?" I ask, hoping she would know. If she was light-complected and could teleport, surely she wasn't a Changer.

She looks off to the trees behind me, reaching far back into her memory. "Star Dweller, I think she called it."

Star Dweller? I absently rub the star-shaped birthmark on my arm. The one my grandmother and I supposedly share.

"But that's all I know. I don't remember what that means, exactly. There weren't many of her kind."

I try not to look disappointed. "Did my mom know?"

She looks at me questioningly.

"About what my grandmother could do?"

"Not sure, but I would think so. He told her everything else."

I nod. My dad never hid anything from my mom. Not that I knew of.

"But that's why I'm wanting you to go with Luxxe," she adds. "If anything bad happens, you can teleport everyone back here."

"I can teleport people?"

"According to your grandmother."

"But I don't even know how to control it."

She rubs my arm lovingly, gives me an apologetic smile. "If I could help you with that, I would. Maybe use what happened the other day and try to recreate it?"

I huff a laugh. "Be attacked by a boar?"

She gives me a *don't be silly* look. "You know what I mean."

I guess.

"Look," she says, looking back to the cabin, "Think about it. You've heard what everyone has to say, and nobody will blame you if you decide not to go. But please consider the advantage you'll give your friends if you do."

I sigh, running my fingers through the tangled ends of my braid.

"And Jacks is obviously supportive of you going."

Spectacle

"Obviously," I mutter.

She kisses my cheek and gathers me into a long hug. "Just think about it, please," she says, a final, desperate plea to ensure her son's safety.

I bite back my immediate refusal, and I'm not sure why. Am I already caving? It feels wrong to go against my first instinct of staying here, but what if I really could make a difference if things go sour? What if I could be my friends' failsafe? There's still the pesky little detail of being able to control my ability. I'd have to work on it and see if it's possible. On the bright side, though, at least now I know I'm not some freaky superhero. My ability is genetic.

"I'll think about it," I finally concede, and she wilts into me, that one ray of hope lifting pounds of worry from her motherly shoulders. I'm sure, after today, they weighed an intolerable amount.

"Thank you," she breathes. "Thank you, thank you, thank you."

The following days are filled with the agonizing responsibility of making an impossible choice — stay with Jacks or go with Luxxe. Two weeks will pass before I know it, and the past three days have flown by already. I only have eleven days left.

But I'm still stuck on this one not-so-simple point — can I even control my ability? Would I be able to help if they need it? And in truth, I'm a little scared to try. Last time, I awoke with a sprained knee, which is thankfully better after a few days of rest, but still, I can't afford to injure myself again.

I've decided to suck it up and try, though. It's the only way to make up my mind.

I look back to the cabin and see that Jacks is still sitting with Maggie as she weaves a basket. They assume I'm down here by the river to take a quick bath, but I have other plans in mind. I dip a toe into the chilly water and shiver, then think of the poem I've been reciting since my last talk with Maggie — *The Road Not Taken*.

It suits my predicament so well — me standing at a crossroads.

I count to three and jump, submerging myself all at once. I yelp from the biting cold, bubbles trickling up to the surface, pins and needles prickling all over. *Dang, it's cold,* but this is the only way I could convince myself to try this. The other thing that kept me from trying it again was remembering how the heat tore at me from the inside. I'm hoping the icy water will balance it out.

We'll see.

Shaking, I close my eyes, coaching myself through it. I visualize the boar again, teeth clacking, eyes flared and angry. He's coming at me like a steam engine and I'm backed against the tree.

Tingles swirl in my chest.

I think it's working.

The tingles roll out to my limbs, consuming me, but I stick with it and focus on the numbing fear. The boar's charging. I could die.

Fire bursts to life where the tingles started, and I want to gasp, but can't. Part of me wants to quit, the fire nearly paralyzing me all over again. It roils and rages against the cold around me, crackling like ice on an ember. I was wrong... the water is making it worse.

Stick with it, Mira.

The boar nears, and I close my eyes to brace for the impact. *On the riverbank again*, my thoughts chant, trying to direct my ability.

His footsteps are seconds from me.

On the riverbank!

Darkness claims me, and I'm gone.

My chest is tight like someone's sitting on it, and I want to scream and swat at them to get off, but I can't move. Like before, I can't do anything. Paralysis must be part of the process.

I give it a minute, then try to wiggle my fingers. Nothing. Still numb.

I'm then acutely aware I'm not breathing. My heart thuds weak and slow. Something's different this time. Something's wrong.

Spectacle

Panic blossoms inside me. Oh, God. What did I do? *Move*, I tell myself, concentrating so hard blood vessels must be bulging at my temples. *Move!*

I slowly feel my arms again and push to roll to my side. My chest aches with the movement, and I heave. Water pours from my nose and mouth immediately, and I choke and cough and sputter until it's all out and I'm left with a burning throat.

What the hell?

Feeling floods my body with a final rush, and I clamber to a sitting position, sucking in as much air as I can between coughs. Jesus... I nearly drowned.

I glance back to the house. Maggie and Jacks are still blissfully unaware.

Sluggishly, I lie back for a moment. My friends almost found me dead on the riverbank. After everything, after all we've survived, I almost killed myself. I choke out a hysteric laugh. *Idiot.*

But on the bright side, I did it. I was able to summon my ability.

Just no more water, I tell myself.

When I'm finally ready to move again, I strip down and wrap a cloth around me. I move to face the house again and watch Maggie and Jacks. He's laughing at something she said, and she pulls him into a hug. The imagery calms me and gives me a surge of reassurance. Maybe he really will be okay if I leave.

Their moment is over, and she helps him stand and move to his mat. From this distance, it's all the more apparent how weak and frail he's gotten.

And he's only going to get worse.

Grief clenches my heart. Maybe he's right. Maybe this mission is about more than clearing our fathers' names. A better future might be in store for him. For all of us. A future we were robbed of.

A new feeling claims me — something bold and unwavering. Something I see in Jacks' spirit, and Luxxe's and Blythe's and everyone else's, but had been missing in my own — a steely determination to make these bastards pay.

With my newfound courage in tow, I make my way to the house, my next words poised on the tip of my tongue: "I'm going."

I've chosen my path.
I shall be telling this with a sigh
Somewhere ages and ages hence:
Two roads diverged in a wood, and I –
I took the one less traveled by,
And that has made all the difference.

END BOOK ONE

Next in the series:

Spectacle, Part Two

Coming September 2018
Join SJ's mailing list herhe: https://www.sjpiercebooks.com/join-my-vips/ to get an email when released!

Loved Spectacle, Part One? I would love to hear from you!
Follow the links to leave a review on one of the online retail sites
and tell me what you think.
Visit: https://www.sjpiercebooks.com/series/

About the Author:

Susan James Pierce has a degree in Marketing Management, works for a Fortune 500 company in Atlanta, Georgia, and devotes her precious spare time to writing Paranormal, Sci-fi, and Romantic Suspense novels.

Please visit: https://www.sjpiercebooks.com/join-my-vips/
and sign up for her mailing list or subscribe to her blog if you'd like to hear when new books come out!
For a listing of her available books, visit:
https://www.sjpiercebooks.com/series/

Find her on Facebook at: https://www.facebook.com/SJPiercebooks

Other Titles Available from this Author

Captivate Me
By S.J. Pierce

All seventeen-year-old Kathrin Walsh wanted when she transferred to a school for the Gifted was to feel accepted and normal, and she does... mostly. But when dreams of another boy make her question her relationship, kids go missing, and she learns something troubling about what she is and why her future will forever be altered, she quickly realizes that 'normal' is only an illusion, and that love can walk a fine line between captivating and maddening, or even worse - it can make you abandon all trace of reason. Love can be deadly.

From the bestselling author of the Alyx Rayer Chronicles, comes a refreshingly different Young Adult series with plenty of love, suspense, and a new take on the Paranormal.

Recommended for readers 16 and up due to mature content.

Fight for Me
By S.J. Pierce

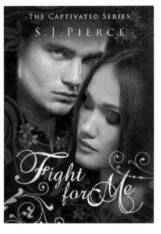

A fresh start - something Kat and Gabriel thought they would find when they left their pasts behind at Midland Pines High and moved to a compound for hybrids. Or at least safety from a witch seeking revenge. But... that's all changed. Thanks to a flirty hybrid hell-bent on winning Gabriel's attention, the terrifying visions of another prophetic Gifted, and the strange and worrisome behavior of one of their closest friends, Kat finds herself fighting for things that had once come so easily, including her relationship with her soulmate. And now she's afraid.

IRIS
By S.J. Pierce

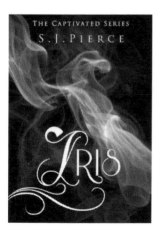

Set before the events in Book One of the Captivated Series, Iris explores the depths of family bonds, new bonds, and the lengths a person would go to save the life of a dying sibling. In this novella, get to know Iris and her two sisters more intimately, as well as Gabriel, the first angel-human hybrid who agrees to live under her protection.

Shine with Me
By S.J. Pierce

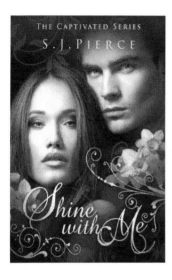

The darkness is coming...

After Lilliana threatens to come back and extinguish everyone at the compound, their leadership decides to take a final stand against the woman whose family has been terrorizing them for years.

In this last installment of the bestselling Captivates series, follow Kat and Gabriel as they help prepare for battle against a conjurer who'd become darker than anyone could have fathomed. Will their love be enough to shine through it?

Lilliana
By S.J. Pierce

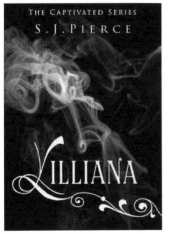

The last living LaRoux sister is pissed and out for revenge. In "Lilliana," the second and final novella to the Captivated Series, follow the brazen, immortal dark conjurer as she sets out on a quest to make her sisters' killers pay.

Other Titles Available from Foundations, LLC

Jasper: Book One – The Guardian League
By T.K. Lawyer

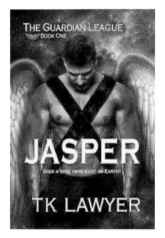

Tatiana seeks rare, coveted treasure: a strong, loving, committed male she can respect, be proud of and become her full-fledged partner. She has sought this elusive prince among men, her own personal champion but instead found many, many frogs and quite a few toads. Does her hero exist on Earth, or did she miss her opportunity? Jasper isn't seeking a mate. His only intention is to rescue Tatiana from a fatal car accident, but he finds himself drawn to her in ways he can't explain. She's a rare, precious gem and there's no turning back for him. He must know her and introduce himself in some sort of "human" fashion, at some sort of "human" event, for he is not of Earth. Once Tatiana finds out Jasper's true identity, will she accept and trust him? Will Tatiana allow herself to enter into a permanent, loving relationship with an unearthly but powerful being who only wants to adore and protect her?

Centurion: Book Two – The Guardian League
By T.K. Lawyer

Centurion has it all. A talented charge, ladies at his disposal for a single encounter or more and access to all the coffee he wants once he lands on Earth. Plus, he's second in command of the volunteer band of angels called the Guardian League. The one thing he never wanted was an intimate relationship with a human beyond the usual angel-charge boundaries. So when he finds a woman as strong and hot as the human beverage that tickles his fancy, what else can he do but pursue her until he figures out what to do with her. April loves her enticing, hunky angel but he's a lot to handle. He's cocky, unpredictable but most of all… incorrigible. What is she to do with a male who lives life by his own schedule? Can April and Centurion form a compromise and allow love to bind them together? Or will Centurion's inability to commit wedge them apart, forever?

EVIN
By A.S. Crowder

Eva has never seen the Forest of Evin, but her fate and the fate of the Forest may be intertwined.

Sinister forces seek to pull the Forest apart, and Eva may be the only one who can save it. Eva must travel between worlds to keep the Forest together…

…but the Forest of Evin thrums with power and the force tearing it apart may not be the only danger.

Pity's Prelude
By Creighton Halbert

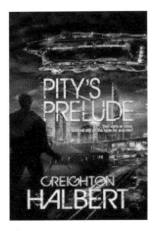

Stephen Bates is desperate. Paid by a foreign superpower to leave Earth and sacrifice his life, he finds that ritual suicide isn't that simple when the planet he lands on erupts into civil war. He and local war hero, Titus Sirocco, struggle to discover who's trustworthy and who's gunning for them. As two different wars rage around them, will Stephen and Titus find what's worth dying for, or will the rebels choose their fate first? And what's with those shapeshifters?

Made in the USA
Columbia, SC
28 April 2022